T0384325

BRIGHT

RED

FRUIT

ALSO BY SAFIA ELHILLO

Home Is Not a Country

BRIGHT RED FRUIT

SAFIA ELHILLO

MAKE ME A WORLD
NEW YORK

MAKE ME A WORLD is an imprint dedicated to exploring the vast possibilities of contemporary childhood. We strive to imagine a universe in which no young person is invisible, in which no kid's story is erased, in which no glass ceiling presses down on the dreams of a child. Then we publish books for that world, where kids ask hard questions and we struggle with them together, where dreams stretch from eons ago into the future and we do our best to provide road maps to where these young folks want to be. We make books where the children of today can see themselves and each other. When presented with fences, with borders, with limits, with all the kinds of chains that hobble imaginations and hearts, we proudly say—no.

Text copyright © 2024 by Safia Elhillo
Jacket art copyright © 2024 by Cienna Smith
Watercolor background by universee used under license from Shutterstock.com

Visit us on the Web! GetUnderlined.com

Educators and librarians, for a variety of teaching tools, visit us at RHTeachersLibrarians.com

Library of Congress Cataloging-in-Publication Data is available upon request.
ISBN 978-0-593-38120-5 (trade) — ISBN 978-0-593-38121-2 (lib. bdg.) —
ISBN 978-0-593-38122-9 (ebook)

The text of this book is set in 11.25-point Adobe Caslon Pro.
Interior design by Michelle Crowe

Printed in the United States of America
10 9 8 7 6 5 4 3 2

First Edition

For my loves. For the poets.

In the tale of Persephone
which should be read

as an argument between the mother and the lover—
the daughter is just meat.

—LOUISE GLÜCK, "PERSEPHONE THE WANDERER"

why did i do it?

why did i lie?

everyone wants me to blame religion, my mother, the country in flames behind us, but i was not an unhappy child. we danced and colored and folded little paper boats to float in the bathtub. we tried our best and locked the doors and installed sensors in the windows. if i am to blame, it is only because i was forever curious, forever climbing onto the sill to peer out the locked window at the lives continuing outside. i was not unhappy, only restless. only hungry to know what we were trying to keep out. it was i who opened the doors, the windows. it was i who let him into the house.

BAD GIRL

all the aunties in the neighborhood love
to remember that i was a sweet kid
laughing & dimpled & affectionate

& these reveries always end with a sigh
as they look at me now, sixteen
& what they call, sorrowfully, *boy crazy*

but ever since i was small i've wanted
to be loved

when it was the aunties i'd reach for
to be embraced, to be kissed, it was fine

but ever since i was small i would lock eyes
with boys on passing buses, in passing cars
& wonder if i could make them love me

though all my life, mama has taken great care
to make sure i never find out

MY NAME

it all started when a boy whose name i wish i did not remember

he & his family long since returned to sudan

told a lie that begat another that begat several more

& in the eye of that storm hissed my name

samira

the littlest exaggeration, intended, i'm sure, to be harmless

to get his friends to stop laughing at his inexperience

his chest puffed out, an untruth forming between his teeth

the insistence that he had, that he does. *with who?* they mocked.

samira

we liked each other, passed notes back & forth

at sunday arabic school, glanced shyly over at each other

at eid gatherings, our hands brushing once at an iftar buffet but nothing more. we barely spoke. never touched. but still

samira

& now he's long gone, years since the story took root

& poisoned my name, so long ago that people barely remember

the lie itself, the story, only the feeling they get when they look

at me, the disgust, the reproach, embarrassment on behalf

of my mother, & also something darker, something gleeful

& carnivorous, sinking into my name, my reputation

& drawing blood, teeth wet & red & shining

samira

BAD GIRL

they always knew i'd turn out like this
everyone now says, ever since some aunties
spotted me holding hands with a boy
at the eid barbecue when we were nine

they knew it, confirmed it when i was twelve
& some aunties spotted me
with a group of boys playing soccer
outside huda's wedding
my bright blue dress streaked with dirt

or three months ago when another rumor started
that i'd let a boy kiss me in the hallway
outside our sunday arabic class, or that i'd kissed
another in the courtyard of the mosque
or another at the movies when we thought no one
would catch us, or another, or another
or an american boy from school, someone swears they saw
at the bus stop one thursday afternoon

here's the story: in sixteen years my lips
have never been kissed, but my name spends years
kissed in every gossiping mouth, kissed
with disapproving teeth, kissed by the threat
of disgrace, of exile, my name kissed
by every whisper, by every shaken head
while i sit inside it, untouched & full
of a wanting i cannot name, of something doused
in gasoline & ready to catch

TAMADUR & LINA

we've known each other
since we came here as little kids

our parents, friends from back home
laughing late into the night at the old stories

while the three of us spoke shyly
to each other in english

now we are sixteen
born weeks apart

& only they understand my doubled lives
the extra set of clothes we each keep in our lockers

denim miniskirts
cropped t-shirts

razors for when we secretly shave
our legs & forearms in the locker room

on weekends we crowd into lina's room
& sometimes swing from her second-floor window

into the oak tree outside
the velvet night below & all its promises

it's summer & we have to find new ways
to hide our contraband

it was tamadur's idea to keep everything
sandwiched underneath our mattresses

& at night i lie above my secret store of treasure
& dream of the wind against my legs

a life lived in the open

LINA

tamadur & i always joke that all our trio's good sense
is housed in lina, our anchor, forever browned by the sun

& smelling of fresh-cut grass, constellation of freckles
dusted across her nose, only visible from up close,

tiniest furrow in her brow as she thinks, measuring out
her every word, turning each thought over slowly in her

forever whirring mind. lina, in sweatpants, her kindness
the kindness of athletes, of kids who've spent their lives

understanding themselves as part of a team, who, when
she isn't referring to us as "we," collects tamadur & me

into a laughing "tam & sam," her smile wide & teeth gapped,
our tallest, her feet eternally outgrowing every running shoe

her sturdy runner's legs, eternal ponytail, her goodness
her sturdy, solid goodness

TAMADUR

the artist formerly known as *tammy* until she spent
the summer before sophomore year reading leather-bound

books with spines the width of my forearm & announced
via online posts & a flurry of text messages to everyone

she knew that she would only answer to her real name
from now on, that mouthful of letters, its percussion a song

from that country we left. tamadur, named for an old-world
poet whose work i've never known enough arabic to read

tamadur, with her enormous name, our historian
maker of our most stomach-cramping laughs

made funnier by her perfect cocktail of our two languages
first to dance, shimmying her shoulders & crooning

old haqeeba songs, two perfect dimples in the smooth
geography of her face. when i think of tam, i think

of symmetry, of our two worlds balanced perfectly
in her two soft hands

FARAH

lina's oldest sister
farah

our cautionary tale
gone for years

though people say
they hear she's still nearby

just on the other side
of town

living in an apartment
with an american boyfriend

& forbidden from seeing her sister
from calling

from ever showing her face
again

farah
our word of warning

of endless cautioning
the line our mothers draw

in the sand
& dare us to cross

that one-word threat of exile
of disgrace

of a whole world
lost

all contained
in one girl's name

i remember her eyes
rimmed with lashes so impossible

that, since childhood, strangers
would pull her mother aside

& whisper that such a young daughter
shouldn't be wearing makeup

& i don't remember much else beyond
the room full of books

the tiny gleam of a ring in her nose
i've all but forgotten the girl herself

& taken her name instead
as all of us have

as a warning

our mothers say *remember farah*
& mean *or else*

don't wear makeup
remember farah

don't talk to boys
remember farah

keep your girlhood small
governable

remember farah
remember how quickly she was made unloved

how quickly she became no one's daughter

RUMORS

one auntie says she saw me at the mall
locked in embrace with a boy

another says she saw me at the diner
miles of bare leg under the table in shorts

an uncle says he saw me getting into
a car after dark

another says he saw me on the bus

pomegranate red on my lips
dark liner along my eyes

at first mama used to yell
to slap her own face & moan

about my reputation, hers, ours
drowning out my every explanation:

i was just hugging my friend & the shorts
are from gym   changed into after

i bled through the day's jeans   the car
is a friend's mother's, dropping me off

after a movie   & the makeup
well, yes, the makeup is mine, but

i didn't see any harm in it & listen
to me why won't you just listen?

THE DREAM

i'm going to be a writer & live
far away from here, in new york city
& never come back
& i'll wear high heels & lipstick

i'm going to be elegant & terrifying
like aunt aida, who lives next door
alone & surrounded by books
shelves stacked floor to ceiling
a glossy wooden ladder perched against them

aunt aida who's watched me my whole life
who gave me books at first
& then paper & pens
listened seriously when i read my poems to her
& afterward said thoughtful things
that made me feel important & heard
aunt aida who never married
tall & made taller by the shoes she wears
clicking along her polished wooden floors
who, these days, is bringing me pamphlets
for colleges
thinks i could get into a program for writing
knows me enough to place the purple one
at the top of the pile
the one right in the heart of new york

NEW YORK

in new york i think i can finally be free

my lips painted daily in a signature red
my eyeliner dark, a little apartment with a closet
full of clothes for all the people i want to be:
ripped tights & heavy boots, towering high heels
a green canvas jacket i saw once in the window
of an army surplus store, which mama would not
let me buy, ever dramatic, telling me she hadn't fled
a military coup for her only daughter to wear clothes
meant for soldiers; all my clothes hanging proudly
in a closet, not hidden in a locker or stuffed under the mattress

& in new york i can finally be an artist, a writer
staying awake until dawn with my new crowd
all poets & musicians & painters, showing each other
what we've made, what we can do, clattering into
train cars & pizza shops. new york where i do not
have to lie, where i do not need an alibi or a second outfit
new york where i do not have a curfew, where maybe
a boy with paint on his clothes will love me, will introduce me
to his friends as *the poet*. new york without my mother.

i love her. i do. but maybe a little space between us
a few states between us will loosen her grip
will release me from the shape of the daughter
she thinks she should have
so i can finally step into the self i've kept small enough
to be hidden

TAMADUR & LINA

a few days into summer break & i wake sweating
the comforter tangled around one foot, my phone
buzzing insistently, steady staccato of text messages
arriving in quick progression that can only mean one thing:
the group text is awake & waiting for me to catch up

i fish blearily under my pillow for the phone
& study the screen with one eye slit open
the other still crusted shut with sleep
messages accumulating in the double digits

TAMADUR:

sam

samira

dude wake up already it's been daytime for hours

need to know RIGHT NOW about the jumpsuit

?????

S

A

M

LINA:

lol she can't actually hear you

also i think i have the jumpsuit

so just come get ready at my house

i rub the sleep from my eyes & watch the screen
fill with the words of my friends, their easy laughter
our whole summer stretched out before us

WHAT I'M NOT ALLOWED TO DO

talk on the phone after 10 pm

talk on the phone for more than an hour

wear eyeliner

go to the public pool

wear shorts

wear a tank top

wear a crop top

wear high heels

wear a swimsuit

wear lipstick

wear my hair down

straighten it

sleep over at tamadur's house because she has brothers

sleep over at lina's house because her sister was disgraced

sleep over at any other house

because mama doesn't know their parents

& because they're not sudanese

lock the door to my room

close the door to my room

use tampons

stay out past 10 pm

go anywhere without telling mama where

& with whom

& the exact activity we'll be doing

("watching a movie," for example, is okay)

("hanging out," for example, is not)

talk to boys

be alone anywhere with any boy or man

even if we're related

call adults by their first names

shave my legs

paint my nails

wear perfume

              ("only for married women")

wear red

              ("only for brides")

wear anything that will hold a lingering gaze

           that will make anyone want to look any closer

MOVIES

over the years we've perfected
our technique   a way to guarantee
two hours' worth of an alibi

> *mama, i'm going to see a movie*
> *with lina & tam*

a theater chosen for its proximity
to where we'll actually be

> *where?*

> *gallery place*

the trick is to choose an actual
movie, its actual showtime

> *when?*

> *3:15*

& we'll take turns looking up
the synopsis

> *what was the movie about?*

> *a superhero travels through time*

& even the reviews

> *how was it?*

> *it was okay. i feel like it spent so much time*
> *explaining but not a lot actually happened*

& today mama chuckles,
her eyes softening

> *my little critic. i loved movies too,*
> *when i was your age. we should*
> *go see one together*

& i work to release myself from the guilt
from the fondness in her eyes

when she is like this i can almost imagine
a simpler version of us

where the hours are currency to be spent
together, instead of contraband i wheedle
from her iron grip

the lie is tiny, hurts no one, is a small price
to pay for my hard-won hours of freedom

TWO SHARP LINES

today we meet up at the big cosmetics store
to try on lipsticks & practice our cat-eye

i stand before one of the mirrors
liner smooth & wet along my eyelids
winged out to a perfect point

dagger with which i wish i could protect
myself from everything that hurts
with which i wish i could carve out
the girl i know i am

cat-eyed & sharp
unafraid & unhidden

looking directly at the world
& inviting it to look back

tamadur sidles up to the mirror beside mine
squeals when she catches my reflection

a vision! an artist! lina come look
what sam did! this symmetry! this precision!

i turn to meet lina's eyes as she approaches
my already-wide smile widening further
at the thick & blocky eyebrows she's drawn
onto her grinning face

want some help with that? i call out
motioning to her brows with my eyes

she cocks one dramatically
why? what's wrong with them?
as tam dissolves into giggles beside me

MAMA

a few days later
i try it again

usually i'll limit the movie thing
to once a week at most

a little space to keep mama
from getting suspicious

but it's the first cookout
of the summer

& i have the most perfect idea
for an outfit

my hair piled up, little jean shorts
big vintage sunglasses

> *mama, can i go to the movies*
> *with lina & tamadur?*

she is standing at the kitchen sink
her back to me, & she is silent for a moment

> *mama?*

> *no*

the word strikes me in the soft
& hopeful part of my chest

>*why not? please?*

>*i will not have a daughter who goes out*
>*every day of the week*

& i feel the prickle of tears forming
at her injustice, her unpredictability

>*it's literally not every day.*
>*just a movie, mama, please?*

she dries her hands on a kitchen towel
& turns to me

>*every day i hear some story*
>*about someone seeing you around,*
>*what you're wearing, who you are with.*
>*you are ruining your reputation*
>*& you are ruining mine.*
>*so like i said, no. today you can stay home*
>*& give me some peace from all the talk*

& i feel frozen by the accusation
wondering who saw me

what they told her, what they think
they saw, but i have no way to defend myself

without incriminating myself first.
all i can do is turn on my heel

& clatter up the stairs to my room
her voice calling up behind me

> *no running*
> *& don't close the door*

TAMADUR & LINA

SAMIRA:

she said no

TAMADUR:

dude what nooooo

did you say we were going to a movie

SAMIRA:

yes literally the same way i asked the other day

it's like she can't decide who she wants to be

she'll be normal for a second

and then it's like she's worried someone is watching her

and she's trying to prove to them that she has me under control

but i'm literally not even doing anything!!!!!!!!!!!!!!

LINA:

ughhhh i'm so sorry that sucks

what's plan b

what if we just come to your house

and actually watch a movie for once lol

SUNDAY SCHOOL

for all her strictness, when i turned sixteen & told mama
i no longer wanted to go to sunday arabic school

(where i wasn't learning much arabic & instead spent every week
being whispered about, the adults gossiping even more
than the kids my age, about my clothes & the way they molded
to my changing body, about the boys who were raised alongside
me like brothers, playmates, kicking a frayed soccer ball in the
grass & climbing trees, whose company became suddenly
& abruptly forbidden, shameful, whose company i still seek
because we're friends, all our lives we've been friends,
but the sight of me tangled in a knot of boys starts a fresh wave
of whispers, that spreading hiss of new names for what i am,
for the shame everyone thinks i fail to feel, but I feel it,
its fingers tight around my throat at every gathering)

with a half-hearted excuse about homework, SATs
early thoughts about college, she surprised me by not

putting up a fight, & i felt the grip loosen, new air
in my grateful lungs

REPUTATION

& it isn't even really religion that governs us
though of course some of the aunties & uncles are
pious in the expected ways, seen so often at the mosque
that i'm not sure they don't sleep there

but the religion we really practice is the religion
of reputation   fear of a deity replaced by fear
of each other   the whispers   the rumors
the disgrace   the brittleness of a family's good name
of a family's honor   the brittleness of the girls
who hold it in our clumsy hands

RELIGION

i think no one will believe me
but i do. believe, i mean. i do.

i'm sure the aunties would scoff
& roll their eyes if they heard me

point out the tightness
of my jeans

the memory of red
along my lips

but when i recite the words
to myself, alone in my room

something in the sounds
the words make

makes something ancient
stir in my chest

AUNT AIDA

she's nothing like the other aunties
&, unlike the other aunties, she is
my actual aunt, mama's older
sister, the only member of mama's
immediate family in this country
which might explain their inexplicable
bond, her house next door, the time
they spend together despite the fact
that they have absolutely nothing
in common. i don't know that they
are close, exactly, but they are together
more often than not, eternal click
of aunt aida's high-heeled shoes
her hands manicured & clean of any
wedding ring

i wouldn't even know who to ask
why aunt aida never married. i think
mama would be too loyal to her sister
to divulge, & though aunt aida is always
kind, little glint of approval never leaving
her eyes when she looks at me, part of me
believes she'll think less of me if i ask
if i reveal myself to care about that sort
of thing

& for all the ways she is different from them all
no one talks about her, none of the whispers
that worry my name into a hiss, none of

the names i am called in place of my own.
never any open judgment. maybe they can tell
she's too fancy to care what they think
everything she owns sleek & silver & expensive
the car, the laptop, the audacity of the cream-colored
furniture in her house, no plastic cover on the couch
the clothes tailored sharply to her body like armor.
one day i'll leave this place & though i hope never
to come back, if i do it will be like aunt aida,
untouchable, my success punctuating every click
of my high-heeled shoes, the words dying
in every malicious throat

SECRETS

the first time i changed into a new outfit at school—
my baggy t-shirt & shapeless trousers replaced
with a cropped white tank top & high-waisted
jeans that curved my body into new hips
the look finished with a pomegranate-red lip
& my hair shaken loose—

mazin, whose dad teaches the arabic class on sundays
sidled up to me at my locker & asked
does your mom have anything to say about those jeans?

i squared my shoulders & turned to face him
my heart going percussive in my throat
& spat back *does your dad have anything to say
about that white girl you're dating?*

& now we find a strange peace, all of us,
the kids from sunday arabic school reassembled
every monday into the high school most of us attend together
& our private economy of secrets, our private country
of secrets: the boy who pretends to tutor math after school
but instead makes costumes for the school play, his fingers
deft against the whirring needle of the sewing machine,
the ones who've started dating, the ones who smoke cigarettes
then douse themselves with a thick & suffocating layer
of body spray

& it's not that we're really even friends, most of us
but our siblinghood is enormous, something

more ancient than friendship, our pact unspoken
& powerful as any constitution:

to tell one would mean telling them all

GROUP CHAT

MAZIN:

tomorrow is me and amber's 2 month anniversary

i think baba's getting suspicious

so i need yall to cover for me

LINA:

what exactly is a 2 month anniversary

HAMZA:

the root of the word is "year"

anni-versary

like "annual"

not month-iversary

WIAAM:

hamza don't be that person

no one likes that person

SAMIRA:

ok how many hours do you need

and whats the story

OLA:

can u keep it to two hours

a movie would be the easiest excuse

maybe 3hrs if we say we got dinner after

the rest of us can go to dylan's

AZZA:

no every time we go to dylan's my hair stinks of smoke when i come home

TAMADUR:

maybe its time u start wearing hijab then my sister

MAMA

mama, can i go to the movies
with some of the kids from sudani school?

i hold my breath & send up a quick & silent prayer
that she isn't in one of her moods today

which kids?

tamadur & lina & mazin & hamza

she arches a perfect eyebrow
& studies me suspiciously

you shouldn't be spending so much time with boys

you didn't let me finish! lina & tam & mazin
& hamza & ola & wiaam & azza. only two boys

she considers me for a moment.
i can almost see her deciding which version
of herself to be this time

she's still quiet & i start up a chant in my head
trying to summon by telepathy my easier mother
the one who, when i was little, i thought
was my best friend

(please)   (please)   (please)   (please)   (please)

i watch her battling my newer, harder mother
the one who speaks in the voice of all the aunties
that i think must probably hate me, who seem almost
disgusted by me, my wild hair, my changing body
as if the eyes they draw leave a residue, leave me dirty
as if it's somehow my fault for not remaining a child
forever

please mama

she sighs, shakes her head as if she is somehow
disappointed in herself, & the movement makes
my stomach drop, until she speaks

fine

THE LANDLINE

for years mama didn't have a cell phone
of her own

i was only allowed to get one
when tamadur's & lina's mothers, in turn
worried loudly to mama at the thought
of me riding the metro home alone from school
with no way of being reached

& even now, with our family plan
& our phones like small panes of glass
in our pockets, the screens smudged
with fingerprints, when i picture my mother
i picture her talking loudly, too loudly
into the house phone, like she can throw
her voice to the other continent by sheer volume

the landline, a relic from another time
with its blinking answering machine
its cordlessness the only gesture
toward the present day   ringing early
in the morning with unanswered calls
from bill collectors searching for uncles
long ago returned to sudan

its clumsy heft, mama cradling it
between her ear & right shoulder
as she stirs a bright pot of lentils

every drawer in the house stuffed
with used phone cards, mama rummaging
through the piles for a fresh one
for five more minutes, for a crackling line
stretched across an ocean

MAMA

because i don't remember a time when she was not alone
my mother's beauty is a cruelty

we hadn't been here a full year before my father
couldn't take it anymore, the indignity of immigration

& left. went back home. last i heard he'd remarried & had sons,
his second draft, my mother & i his clumsy practice run

& so she hates to be looked at, hates to be touched
hates so much i sometimes wonder if i might also

be somewhere on that list. sometimes i imagine us
still close, her hands braiding oil into my hair

i imagine everything she might tell me: *i was born
in a big house. my grandfather's, he built it during*

*golden times, date palm years that trickled away
years before i was born. now we are here, & the walls*

*hang heavy with pictures of our dead, bodies that time
loved too jealously. thick-knuckled women who cooked*

*for well-loved men, raised children in the silence,
& in that silence we grew hardened, & in that silence*

i was forged. i was born lonely, & you, my daughter,
were born lonely too, i imagine she'd say

but we don't really ever talk like that
so i write the poem instead

FREEWRITE

pretty girl, he says
not as pretty as my mother, you say
your hair, he says
not as beautiful as my mother's, you say
are those your father's eyes, he asks
it's why she doesn't like me, you say
is that your mother's smile, he asks
i never left my mother's body, you say

FARAH

saturday night & lina's house is quiet
we creak about her room getting dressed
for a party at someone's house
some friend of a friend of a classmate
our lips glossed & hair loose

& in a jolt of electricity we turn to lina's mother
filling the doorway with her anger   *what are*
you wearing?   where did you get these clothes?
where do you think you are going   painted
like this?   she turns to face lina   *not again*

i won't lose you like i lost farah
& turns at the break in her voice
clicks the door shut behind her
before the tear can fall

AUNT AIDA

before leaving i wash my face of makeup
& pull my oversized t-shirt back on
the crop top hidden carefully back
underneath lina's mattress

the night deflated, i walk home
& shut the door gently behind me
expecting mama to be already asleep
but i find her in the living room talking
in murmurs with aunt aida, who is showing her
something on her thin silver laptop

& just as i think they haven't seen me
mama looks up & beckons me over.
samira, your aunt thinks this program will be helpful
for college, for helping with scholarships.
& just as i begin to roll my eyes at whatever
science tutor or math camp they've come up with
the screen catches my eye
the words sweet as any song
printed boldly across:

TEEN POETRY WORKSHOP
the start date a month from today
& my face breaks into a grin.
i look to aunt aida
& she is wearing one to match

SUMMER

what i love most is summer

the long, languid days at the waterfront

at the movies & their delicious clean cold

piling onto the grass with a mini speaker
& melting ice cream

what i love most is that feeling

the one i don't know what to name

that i can only call *summer*

the closest i can get to freedom

TAMADUR

sitting beside tamadur on the bleachers
my legs prickly with heat inside their jeans

tam's face is slick with sweat, but the architecture
of her cheekbones makes it look like highlight

light pooling in the high points of her face.
she uncrosses her legs & uses the skirt

of her bright red sundress to fan herself
glint of a fake nose ring in her left nostril

sam, how are you not melting in those?
& i sigh. *you should have seen my other outfit,*

it was perfect. i mourn the matching crop top
& shorts i'd had on first, their sunny shade

of summer yellow, contrast of the pomegranate lip.
then mama's key in the door, hours after she was meant

to be at work, back for her forgotten purse.
& tam, when i tell you i've never changed so fast—

i was in a whole new outfit before she'd made it
up the stairs, & before i could change back she was like,

i'll give you a ride to lina's game, but we have to leave
right now, & i was going to be late otherwise,

so here i am, wearing jeans & long sleeves
in ninety-degree weather

she clucks out a noise of sympathy
as she rummages through the enormous canvas tote

she uses as a purse, emerges with a full jar of pickled turnips
hot pink in their liquid, unscrews the cap, & goes right in

with her fingers. *you want?* she pronounces around the mouthful
of bright acid & salt, & i giggle, filling with a rush of tenderness

for her perfect strangeness. *you're such an auntie, you can't*
even help it, even in that little dress. & she looks down

at the still life she's made, bright pink turnips against
the bright red dress, her laugh braiding into mine

TAMADUR

i tell her about the poetry workshop, & she squeals
with excitement, already rattling off the names
of famous sudanese writers & calling me their child

her face grows even brighter as a thought arranges
itself in her head

*okay so, i've had this idea forever—there's just so much
cool sudanese art stuff that none of us ever get to see,
except for the old uncles that sing at people's weddings,*

*& i want to put a show together, something to showcase
this new generation of artists we have that aren't taken
as seriously. like, did you know mazin plays guitar?*

*& hamza does these really cool paintings that we can frame
& display, & wiaam makes jewelry that she can sell,*

& you, my star, here she places a hand on each of my shoulders
& looks me mock-seriously in the eye, *you'll read some poems*

*& wow us with your gifts, & it'll be amazing! i'll find a space,
so stay tuned for the date.* & now she's rummaging in her canvas sack

again for her phone, mumbling happily to herself about catering
& tickets, & i warm in anticipation of the stage, the microphone,
the whole room listening to the sound of my voice

TAMADUR & LINA

TAMADUR:

do you think i could do my event at the mosque

like is that allowed

LINA:

lol probably not

unless you want to fit all those people into the women's section

SAMIRA:

you mean the basement

or the parking lot

TAMADUR:

ok good point

also is hamza cute or do i only think that bc he's an artist

SAMIRA:

i wanna go to that pool party

LINA:

ok but what happens if our hair gets wet

like how will we explain that

should i just wear a swim cap

SAMIRA:

lina what

a SWIM CAP

TAMADUR:

lina ur my one true love

don't ever change

and also don't you dare wear a swim cap to this party

TROUBLE

a week after being caught
dressing for that party

lina's mother calls mine
makes it seem like it was all

my idea, my fault, & just when
it seems like she's built her whole

case around that old rumor
the old whispers, in addition

to the fact that i sometimes
wear lipstick, bright red

& her daughter does not
would never—

she forwards mama a photo
as evidence that i am *a bad girl*

that i am corrupting her pure
& precious daughter.

ever dramatic, mama prints out
the photograph & tosses it into my lap

silent & gathering clouds
like a brewing storm

it's a photo i used to love: i'm at the park
smiling up from the grass in a pile of friends

& then i see what she sees

a boy's hand draped messily
over my bare shoulders

in their tank top

another's head
on my bare thighs

in their shorts

the clothes my mother doesn't know
i even own

the clothes i know
i'm not allowed to wear

SUMMER

what's actually scary is that mama
doesn't yell at all

instead her voice is hard & quiet & sure.
if i hear of any bad behavior, samira,

you are staying here forever,
none of this new york. i won't

pay for any application to any college
that isn't here. you have the rest

of the summer to change my mind.
& in the set of her jaw i watch

my entire summer turn to ash
leaving a sour taste in my mouth

my heart beating so intently
i can almost see it through my shirt

& i swear i mean to stay silent
until she finishes

but i can't help but squeak out
& the poetry workshop?

& for a moment i think she might hit me
as something flashes in her eyes

& then settles *your aunt aida already*
paid for it, so you'll go

she's agreed to drive you there
& bring you home right after

& some of the pressure
in my chest begins to lift

until she holds her hand out
for my phone

TAMADUR & LINA

tamam_al_tamam:

ok i was right hamza is definitely cute

AND

he messaged me just now being like

we should hang out sometime

that's a date right?

ARE WE DATING???

lina1234567:

lol you went from zero to arranged marriage so quick

also sam are you ok

i'm really sorry about my mom

you know how she is

i tried to explain to her but she's so intense now since farah

but i swear i told her it wasn't your fault

you probably got ur phone taken away

but hopefully you can see this on the computer?

xo_samira_07:

it's not ur fault

mama honestly loves to believe anything bad about me

but anyway she let me keep the computer

aunt aida convinced her i'd need it for poetry workshop

i don't think mama even knows what social media is

so she didn't think to make it part of my grounding

but no phone and no going out

so this is where i'll be the rest of the summer lol

:(

SUMMER

it's been almost a week & my days
are indistinguishable from one another

mama turns the air-conditioning off before
she leaves for work

to keep me from sleeping in too late
so i begin every day coated in sweat

i pour myself a bowl of the nasty bran flakes
that are the only american cereal mama deigns to buy

& i add heaping spoonfuls of sugar until
it's somewhat edible

mama calls me on the landline every hour
on the hour, to make sure i haven't gone anywhere

i fold myself onto the sofa, cereal bowl balanced
on the arm of the couch & a book open against my knees

i devour my library books, sometimes two whole
novels in a single day, while steadily working

my way through the contents of the fridge,
freezer, & pantry. i read a big book of greek myths

persephone stolen from her mother by a man
from the lower world, the red fruit that tethers her there.

& for the first few days i try to avoid
the computer, the endless scroll of photos

of my friends having a summer without me
but on the fifth day, i give in

FREEWRITE

in the myth
everyone knows
what the mother wants
what hades wants

but none of them tell us
about the girl
persephone

were any of the choices
her own

or was she only taken
from one captor
by another

ONLINE

so now i'm spending my summer on the computer

watching videos, clicking through pictures

of my friends bobbing up from swimming pools

& when i can't take it anymore, the longing

i exit those windows & load up the message boards

where i've been reading poems all week, nothing like

the drowsy nature poems i yawn through in school, but poems

about our neighborhoods, about love & longing & anger

that's where i see him first

horus, i mean

that's where i first saw him & fell

HORUS

i guess i'll start by saying that he is beautiful, obviously
a face that makes me want to draw, to paint

jawline to be diagrammed with a ruler to capture its architecture
his lips, muscular & always puckered as if for a kiss

he is unlike any of the boys i know in the way he adorns himself:
pendants, rings encrusted with ancient-looking stones

hair like a bonfire, the dense coil of an afro
tipped with little free-form dreadlocks

i watch the video of him over & over
& wish i were the girl from the poem

the one he calls *queen,* calls *goddess*
the way he shapes each word from his perfect mouth

his lower lip cracked & earnest until he sucks it in
& it reemerges, glistening with saliva

& my body feels emptied of all its bones

WHAT I LOVE

anonymized by usernames, these hours
feel more real than any of my offline interactions all summer:

sitting wooden & silent with mama over dinner
even tamadur & lina feeling far away & abstracted

the self-naming makes me brave
& i post my first poem:

arimasamira:

what i love

dead artists i
have never met

pairs of
hands attached
to long-forgotten
bodies

silence and my
own echoing darkness

lipstick pressed
to the riverbed of
the unkissed mouth

a map
a painted teapot

a mother to whom i
will never belong

the saxophone's loneliness

my border-state body

and summer

HORUS

i thrill at the handful of notifications
my poem has already received

some hearts, a few comments
a few people even reposting it
onto their own pages

& the blinking envelope icon on my dashboard

i click & there he is
his messages lowercase & informal
& twisting my stomach
with an excitement so delicious
it feels like torture

eyeamhorus:

beautiful

the poem, i mean

but also you

where you from?

i'm horus by the way

arimasamira:

hi :)

i'm samira

i'm from dc

u?

eyeamhorus:

everywhere

but mostly new york

where you from originally though?

i really love ur look

arimasamira:

sudan

in east africa

right under egypt

eyeamhorus:

so you're a pharaoh :)

arimasamira:

not exactly lol

sudan is its own thing

but!

khartoum, where my mom is from

is where the two niles meet

and become the big nile that goes up into egypt

                                          eyeamhorus:

                                    "where the two niles meet"

                                                i love that

                                    you should put that in a poem

& i spend the rest of the night
lobbing messages back & forth
until finally, he sends

                                          eyeamhorus:

        eyelids going heavy, beautiful girl. i'll be dreaming of you

& i click out of the window, thrilling
feeling like a strummed guitar
so loud & awake i may never sleep again

2

[He] saw her, loved her, carried her away—
Love leapt in such a hurry!

—OVID, *METAMORPHOSES*

BREAKUP

i've never been in love, or in
a relationship, never really even had
a crush who liked me back
until (maybe) (hopefully) horus

but when i hear all the songs
about heartache, a song about
a breakup, the only one i can think of
is my mother. someone i used
to know. our private war. here,
across from me at dinner, bustling
about the kitchen behind me while
i wash the dishes afterward, honeyed
scent of her perfume oil like a ghost
from a time that found me nestled
into her side, my hand clasping hers
her fingers tugging expert partings
into my hair

i steal glances at her now & it isn't
that i don't know her anymore
so much as i don't know that younger
easier version of myself who knew
how to love her, how to make her
love me, her soft hands cupping
my head, applying the vaseline
to my scrubbed face, quick kiss
on the forehead when she was done

it used to be enough, to be her girl,
her only daughter, only other person
in this house. until it wasn't. until
i awoke to new hungers, the whole world
in its colors tempting me like fruit
like the seven seeds of pomegranate
that ruined persephone. my outstretched
hand before me. looking back to see
the small life we share, so small i cannot
believe it ever fed us both. i want the world,
all of it, & it is on the other side
of our front door, outside my mother's
house &, it seems, outside my mother's love.
& i don't think she ever forgave me for leaving
her behind

HORUS

i've been writing nonstop
poem after poem spilling
from some unlocked place
& every time i post, within minutes
a blinking envelope on my screen
& a message from horus   *beautiful*

i spend an hour on my makeup
just to send him a single photo
sharp line along my lids
lips pomegranate red
my nefertiti he calls me
& i'm too starry-eyed to correct him

& now my days have a new shape
my books gather dust
as i settle at the computer each morning
hoping he hasn't forgotten me in the night
& without fail, every morning, he is there

eyeamhorus:

hey beautiful girl

HORUS

eyeamhorus:

what does your name mean?

i don't actually know the answer
& i can't believe i never even once thought
to ask mama, or tamadur
but i don't want to disappoint him
so i do a quick online search
a little grateful that we aren't having
this conversation in person

arimasamira:

it's weird i don't super understand it

it has something to do w good conversation

the root apparently means "to spend the night talking"

but idk that word in arabic

and then "samira" is like

"companion with lively conversation"

but in the evening

"when the sky is clear and the stars are shining"

it's hard to translate

lol

incredibly corny i know

i didn't choose the name ok!!!!

i'm just the one that has to live with it

eyeamhorus:

i don't think it's corny at all

i think it fits you perfectly

beautiful samira with the beautiful name

i love "when the sky is clear and the stars are shining"

i might borrow it for a poem lol

here's my phone number, by the way

if you're ever up for a night talk :)

arimasamira:

i don't have a phone right now actually

it's a long story

but yes i'd love a night talk soon :) :)

HORUS

i quickly become addicted
to his attention, & he supplies it
abundantly, hours on the computer
exchanging messages late into the night

he wants to know about everything
i do all day, who i saw, what i wore
as if my every thought & action are interesting
& it's intoxicating, to be cared about like this
to have someone want so badly to know me

& in his open wanting i am able to openly
want him back, no games between us
no need to minimize our feelings

& this must be what it feels like to be
in love, i know it, though i'm too shy
to say it so early, but i relish how stunned
he also seems by our spark

eyeamhorus:

i've never connected this quickly with anyone

i've never felt like this about anyone else

maybe it's because ur a poet too

so it's like we connect on every level

eyeamhorus:

you're such an old soul, samira

arimasamira:

lol who r u calling old

:)

eyeamhorus:

i feel like our hearts are twins

you know what i mean?

like our hearts are the same age

tamam_al_tamam:

hellooooooooo

earth to sam

girl where are u

lina1234567:

tam she's grounded remember

tamam_al_tamam:

no i mean like EMOTIONALLY

where u at

it's not like you to leave us on read like this

eyeamhorus:

hey beautiful girl

so i've been thinking

you should be careful about posting poems on here

people might take them without giving credit

it's happened to me before

i would hate to see that happen to you

HORUS

the days pass & we fall
into a rhythm
horus & i
he's on tour
the time zone changing
every few days

but always there to send
a flurry of messages back
& forth every night
to call me *beautiful girl*
& tell me
about life on the road
to send me songs
& recommend books
all of which i devour

& i'm writing every day
though not posting as much
ever since he told me
to be careful about the forum
but promised to read
everything i write

if i send it directly to him
so i do
& he does

HORUS

his poems are beautiful

i spend hours
down the rabbit hole of the internet
watching all the videos

the oldest one just under seven years old
though there haven't been any new videos
in over a year

arimasamira:

you hear this probably every day lol but i still have to tell u

i love your poems so much

would u ever be down to show me some of your writing?

something the rest of the world hasn't seen yet :)

eyeamhorus:

why don't you show me some more of yours?

or, even better, why don't you write me something?

& before i can chicken out i am typing
& erasing & typing again, & the poem emerges

& before i can change my mind
i've clicked *send:*

horus

i think i met all the
wrong ones before
you and i think they
ruined me but i
think you're really
handsome the way
a map is handsome,
with skin wide open
soaked in the whole
world's ink. i
think i'm done pulling
paint off the walls i
think i want to read
you the names of
every city that ever
burned down, i think
we'd like it there

HORUS

when he doesn't respond right away i start to panic
i start typing again

arimasamira:

it's ok if u don't like it i just kind of pulled it
out of nowhere lol don't read too much into it

minutes pass
each one dragging its sharp claws
along my stomach
& still nothing

arimasamira:

u still there?

& just as i am about to click the window shut
& throw myself into bed to cry
the window lights back up

                                        eyeamhorus:

                                            beautiful

                                            wow

                                            samira

i don't even know what to say

this is the most beautiful thing i've ever read

no one's ever made me feel this way

& i feel like i could float up out of my chair
i start typing back immediately

arimasamira:

wow i'm so glad

you took long enough

i was convinced you hated it

& his next message comes
& i feel shot through with electricity
with purpose

his next message reads simply:

we should meet

THE PLAN

he'll be in town in a few days
to feature at the local open mic
at a bookstore & café i've been to
with aunt aida
& i have to find a way to go

i wouldn't miss it for the world
for new york
for college or the poetry workshop
or anything
but i know i'm being stupid

so i call aunt aida
& of course i don't say anything
about horus & tell her only
that there's an open mic
& i'm dying to go
i tell her i've been writing nonstop
that i want to try to read
some poems out loud
to get them ready for the workshop

& i squeal with joy when she agrees

AUNT AIDA

aunt aida rings the doorbell & i rush out
before mama can change her mind
turning back to wave at her as she peers
through the curtains to make sure it's really
aunt aida outside

& as i fasten my seatbelt, aunt aida, her voice
apologetic, is saying
i actually have to get back
to the office, i'm so sorry.
but i'll drop you off & pick you up as soon
as it's done, i promise. i'm so sorry i won't get
to hear you read. you look great, by the way,
but are you wearing your mother's perfume oil?
not to be your aunt about it, but that's for grown
women, you know?
& i am working every
muscle in my body to keep my face from breaking
into a smile
or my body into an excited dance
instead i nod seriously
& thank her for going out of her way to drive me

OPEN MIC

the room is crowded
charged with anticipation

a long line forming at the stage
for the sign-up sheet

i join the line before i can change my mind
& write my name halfway down the list

scanning the room through the corner of my eye
for horus, the now-familiar shape of his hair

but i don't see him
instead, with a jolt of recognition
i see farah, lina's exiled sister

i recognize her first by her eyes
smoky, with those heavy lashes lined brightly in blue

a clipboard in her hand
adjusting the microphone fluently
like she's done it a thousand times

she catches me staring & winks.
the first commandment for all performers:
righty tighty, lefty loosey

adjusts the mic stand one more time to demonstrate
& before i can ask if she recognizes me

she turns to greet someone
& my stomach grows warm with excitement
when i see who it is

it's him & he smells like sandalwood
his arms shining with some kind of oil

a little shorter than i imagined
but just as beautiful as all the pictures
all the videos

i try to catch his eye & when i fail
i slink, embarrassed, into a seat
& wait for the show to start

OPEN MIC

when my name is called i think, for one frantic moment,
that i'll pretend i didn't hear
& slip away from the dimly lit room
to wait in the bookstore outside for aunt aida to get me
but i don't know how else to let horus know i'm here

so i rise & make my awkward way to the stage
unsure how to hold my arms or how to arrange my face
& when i reach the stage the microphone is too high.
i fumble with it for a moment, & i think it's stuck

i look, panicked, to farah, who is hosting the show,
& she mouths *lefty loosey* & with a twist to the left
the microphone slides down toward me
& with a twist to the right i lock it into place

i close my eyes & take a breath
hands clutching my notebook
shaking & sweating
before i settle into a sudden calm
a sudden internal quiet.
i take another breath & begin
what i love: dead artists

i have never met
pairs of hands attached to long–
forgotten bodies . . .

& when i'm done i feel dazed
like i've just broken my head
through the surface of water
& i take large gulps of air
as i work my way back to my seat
sitting down right as farah begins
to introduce horus

HORUS

he performs all the poems i've come to love
from watching the videos
but in person they are even more electric
& take new shapes as the audience around me
hums in admiration
snapping & clapping & stomping their feet

he's mesmerizing
the poems memorized & fluent in his perfect mouth
his hands floating up & around
& making shapes like a conductor
his voice is rich & deep & makes me think
of something caramelized

i catch myself mouthing along to the poems
& then he's done & the spell breaks & everyone
around me is rising to their feet for a standing ovation
& from the stage he catches my eye & waves
& i feel a little light-headed
all the blood rushing to my face

FARAH

horus was, of course, flooded with fans
the moment he left the stage
& i have to keep an eye out for aunt aida's car
so i slip away & browse the shelves
of the bookstore while i wait
already composing a message in my head
to send to horus later

until i am enveloped by the dark & velvet scent
of sandalwood
a hand at my waist
a voice in my ear

it's you

& i turn to him
as my entire body hums with his attention.
i put a hand up to his chest & smile

& it's you

& through the window i see the familiar silver
of aunt aida's car arrive.
i peel myself reluctantly away.
i'm so sorry, but my ride's here.
you were amazing, by the way.
one corner of his mouth
pulls up into a smile.
you're amazing

& before i can get myself into any
more trouble i squeak out
okay, bye!
& scurry out toward the door
where i am intercepted by farah.
hey, really great job tonight. she seems
to realize i'm on my way out, & a new
urgency enters her tone

hey, also, real quick, aren't you one
of my sister's friends? lina's friend? sorry to be
so direct but that makes you, what, sixteen?
you should know that horus is at least twenty-five.
she says this with a slight furrow in her brow
& i immediately feel my defenses sharpen
the collective brain beneath my brain reciting
all the reasons i shouldn't trust her
shouldn't be seen with her

until i return to myself & feel
my stomach tighten with guilt
feeling somehow like i should apologize to her
but i am already shaking her hand off my shoulder
& turning away.
i have to go, my aunt's here.
i stumble out into the night
my head reeling

in the car i answer aunt aida's questions distractedly
yeah it was great, it was good, thanks again.
& at home i click open the computer
a blinking envelope on the screen
a message from him sent five minutes ago

eyeamhorus:

what's your day like tomorrow, beautiful girl?

any time for me?

AGE

we've never talked about our ages
in terms of actual numbers, horus & i,
not really, though he occasionally
will repeat what he said about me
being *an old soul,* & ever since
the one time he said that he felt
like *our hearts are twins, our hearts
are the same age,* i've been floating
on a cloud of that sweetness

& so what if he's older? before him
i didn't know how little i had
in common with boys my age
how little we really had to talk about—
school, our parents, homework, parties.
with horus i can talk about books,
about literature, & he sends me music
& is a proper artist, an actual professional
poet, & in learning about his life
his sold-out shows, his endless tour
i see the shape of a life i could want
for myself, the artist i want to become
that i am becoming right now, in real
time, as i grow into the version
of myself that he sees in me

TAMADUR & LINA

xo_samira_07:

i met someone

a boy

he's a poet

and he's perfect

also lina did u know farah hosts the open mic

at bookshelf and mocha

we didn't really get to talk but i saw her

tamam_al_tamam:

so THAT'S where you've been lol

ok tell us everything!!!!!!!!!!

xo_samira_07:

i'm spending the day w him tomorrow

what's a look that says like

i am grown and sophisticated and a serious poet

or something

lina1234567:

she told me she saw you

we don't text really bc i don't want a paper trail for mama

but we email sometimes

xo_samira_07:

she looks great

makes me want to cut my hair

and get a nose ring

and learn to do eye makeup

ok but seriously what should i wear

THE PLAN

the next morning i lie alert in bed
listening as my mother gets ready for work

finally the door clicks shut behind her
& i bolt out of my crumpled sheets
stopping to borrow some more of her perfume oil

sending up a quick prayer that i don't miss my bus
i click open the message thread

my blood swirling & excited & making it difficult
to type

arimasamira:

meet me at the 15th & chapin entrance?

across the street from the meditation center

i have exactly eight hours until she's home

& plan to spend every minute i can in the meantime
sprawled out on the grass in malcolm x park

with horus & a blanket & a stack of books
a portable speaker & two bottles of iced tea

HORUS

he is standing at the entrance
lounging against a low stone wall
dressed simply in dark denim, bright
sneakers, a white t-shirt cut close
to his body, calligraphy of tattoos
spilling out beneath each cotton sleeve

his face brightens as he sees me approach
full mouth stretching into a smile
that makes him somehow younger
the boy he must have been once
tiny gap between his two front teeth

& my body forgets its simple mechanics
my feet suddenly clumsy in their walk
the fear of seeming ungraceful in his eyes
making my arms heavy in their ugly swing
at my sides, growing awareness that my quick
bites of breakfast on the way out of the house
have left a thick taste of onion in my mouth

& right as the self-consciousness completes
its cruel lap around my brain, he is two steps
away, then one, & now his arms are around me
& now his heady scent, sandalwood & skin
his lips against my ear, low murmur i barely
catch through the loud rush of blood to my head

but i hear it, i hear him as he says to me
so quietly, as if i am the only one he is ever
speaking to, his voice in my ear

you're so beautiful

THE PARK

we spend hours blissful in the sun
listening to every song he recommends

talking about our lives & everything we love
aching closeness of his right arm next to my left

the electric brush of his sleeve against
my bare shoulder as he reaches to restart the song

& he is so beautiful i could lose the thread
of the conversation & fall into silence studying his face

but his eyes are alert & interested, long-lashed
& intent, concentrating on my every word

he asks me questions, so many i can barely get in
any of my own, as if i fascinate him

as if he is drinking deeply from my every fact
my every detail, nodding along, smiling with his teeth

sheer pleasure of the laugh that startles out of him
& just as i begin to describe my dream of living

in new york, of being a writer
"no ordinary love" starts to play & his eyes

on me have changed   the pupils dilated.
he pulls his lower lip into his mouth

the move i've grown to love   & as it emerges
he leans over   & my world is all sensation

is emptied of everything but his lips & that song
& when i resurface from the kiss i feel out

of breath   like i've been swimming
like i almost drowned but didn't

TAMADUR & LINA

i make it home with time to spare
to change back into sweats

& wash the makeup off my face
& flop onto the couch with a book

before mama gets home
& i look like i've been lying there for hours

i yawn & stretch & rise to help her with dinner
assembling the knife & cutting board

& pile of onions on the counter in front of me
& before i can make the first cut, the doorbell rings

tamadur & lina stand grinning when i open the door
tamadur holding up an enormous foil-wrapped plate

mama said to send these over so i figured lina & i
could invite ourselves for dinner

& i send a pleading look over to mama
who takes the plate & unwraps it

finds it full of tamadur's mother's famous lamb sausages
& with a small smile she agrees

TAMADUR & LINA

after we've eaten & washed & dried every dish
& put them neatly away & brought mama a cup
of tea & two ginger biscuits & left her to watch
her turkish soap operas

we clatter upstairs to my room
mama calling behind us
don't run. & no closing the door
i roll my eyes & turn some music on
to drown out our voices
as i begin to tell them everything

& by the time i've finished recounting the kiss
their eyes are huge
shocked or awed, i can't tell
lina is the first to speak
sam, at the park? anyone could have seen you
& i scowl at her
before we rain all over this, let's be happy for me
for a second? i'm pretty sure i'm in love
& tamadur squeals & asks to see a picture
& when i pull one up on the computer even lina
has to agree that he's beautiful

HORUS

after we've gone through every photo of himself
he's sent me & every photo of him we could find
online, tamadur is fanning herself & pretending
to swoon, but lina's face looks more & more troubled
with every passing moment

i dig my elbow into her side
what's this face? can we try more of like
what tam's doing? tamadur grins at this
her smile so infectious that my own stretches
to join hers, but lina's face is still unsmiling
& serious

lina, seriously, what?

she turns to me, that little crease in her brow
as she continues working out her thought
sam, how old is he? he looks like . . . i don't know,
like an adult? is this okay? to which i roll
my eyes & groan

it's fine, seriously, what kind
of conversations could i even be having
with the boys our age? with horus i feel like
i can be my actual self & care about the things
i actually care about, & he doesn't make me feel
weird about it, & that's more important than
something like age, so how about we leave
the judgment to the aunties & just go back
to being happy for me?

& tamadur is nodding her head
thoughtfully at my words, but lina's face
is stubborn, & for a moment she seems like she's going
to dig in her heels & argue, but she only shrugs

& before any awkwardness can set in, tamadur
fills the silence with her squeals of *saaaaaam*
oh my god, is this a BOYFRIEND!!!!!

A BOYFRIEND

none of my friends have ever had
a boyfriend, so i don't know how
to tell for sure if horus is mine
if it's official, even though we talk
for hours every day, & we've kissed
& he reads my poems & calls me
beautiful & asks about my day
& makes me playlists & sends me photos
of pages of books he's reading that remind
him of me, & it all seems so perfect
that it would be silly to ask him for a label
which might make him think i don't know
what i'm doing, might make him think
too hard about my age, so i will not ask him.

i've spent what feels like my whole life
governed by rules: what to wear, who
to talk to, at what volume, how to sit,
how to eat, what to do with my hair.
but i don't know the rules for this. how
to call him mine. how to be his. what i'm
allowed to ask for. i will not reveal
my ignorance, my sheltering. i will not
reveal myself with my questions

SECRETS

they used to be so small, my secrets—

a few borrowed hours to spend at the mall,
at a party, a few contraband pieces of clothing

they used to be so easy to keep
so easy to hide underneath the mattress

& now i am falling in love, & i can't tell anyone
about it, not really, maybe tam & lina
a little bit, but i haven't been able to forget
lina's troubled face

now i am exactly as i've been painted
by all the rumors: cat-eyed & lipsticked & kissed,

boy crazy, my every waking hour consumed
by thoughts of his voice, his scent, his lips

maybe i don't need to prove the aunties wrong.
maybe i'm becoming who i was always going to be

everyone treats me like a child or a problem, & only horus
can see me, our twinned hearts the exact same age

i'll keep it, this secret, not because i am ashamed
but because it belongs only to me

TAMADUR & LINA

lina1234567:

ur both coming to my game on monday right

or sam are you still grounded

tamam_al_tamam:

i will be there!

mazin and amber are coming too

also can u explain the calendar to me is it just soccer season forever

idk how you can run around in this heat but i support you

xo_samira_07:

omg i wishhhh but my poetry workshop starts monday!

sorry :(

WORKSHOP

the poetry workshop starts today
& i'm grateful to have a reason
to change out of my sweatpants
to be out in the world without the need
for an elaborate alibi

the room is air-conditioned
to the point of freezing
ten of us are seated at individual desks
arranged into a circle

the instructor is running late
& the minutes tick past in a rustling of bodies
as we adjust quietly in our seats
waiting for someone to speak

the door creaks open, & a familiar figure
hurries into the room
those familiar thick-lashed eyes
cropped hair curling tightly around her ears

farah sets a stack of books & papers
onto the remaining empty desk
wipes her shining brow with the sleeve
of a perfectly frayed denim jacket

straightens up & looks around the room with a smile
as i wait for her eyes to alight on my face

FREE

farah's smile visits each of our faces
rests there for a second before moving
to the next point in the circle.
thank you all for coming today,
for helping create this space for all of us.
my name is farah, but the poets call me free.
you're welcome to use either one.
my pronouns are she/her,
& my favorite poet is . . . oof, that one's hard.
okay, top three: patricia smith, kamau brathwaite,
& joyce mansour. which one of you would like
to go next?

one by one i learn the names of the others
each shift down the circle naming new poets
new names to write down
i don't recognize a single one
& the shame starts its warm circling in my chest

the boy seated to my left says *gabriel, he/him,*
& my favorite poets are kwame dawes
& aracelis girmay.
& then it's my turn to speak
the words catch for a moment
i clear my throat & try again
um, hi, samira, she, her, hers,
& my favorite poet is horus.
& something moves like a ripple

across farah's face
barely discernible before she smooths it
back over, smiles again.
great, thanks, samira. who's next?

FARAH

our assignment for next workshop is to bring in a poem
that we love, to talk for ten minutes about what
we notice about the writing, what tools we can borrow
for our own

i raise my hand, & farah calls my name
pronounces it the way we do at home
not *suh-mee-ruh* like i'm used to hearing outside
but *se-mee-ra*, full lilt of the arabic
coursing through its every vowel

i try to swat away the anxieties
creeping into my head:
the secret i'll have to keep from mama
from aunt aida, that farah leads the workshop.
the worry they won't let me keep attending.
the embarrassment at having so much in common
with someone who i've been told for years is *bad*
a bad girl

those same words i hear so often
whispered after my own name

FARAH

workshop comes to a close, & the others
rise in a chorus of scraped chair legs
chattering & pouring out of the room
& before i can join them, farah is standing
over my desk, her face urgent & unsure

samira, before you go, we should talk

i settle back into my chair & look up at her
expectantly, & when she doesn't begin
right away, i hear the nervousness in my own
quiet voice when i tell her aunt aida will be
waiting, that i can't stay long

she takes a breath, sets her mouth
in a determined line, & begins

HORUS

samira, there is so much i need to say to you,
& i know you have to go, so i'll just start
with this: you need to be careful around horus

here she stops, closes her eyes, & takes a long
breath in & out. *actually, what i mean is that*
you need to stay away from horus. he has a really

bad reputation, & you don't need to get mixed up
in all that. i know that maybe you & i don't really
know each other anymore, but i'd do the same

for lina, i still think of you as being like my little
sister, & if anything happened to you, i wouldn't
be able to forgive myself

& her voice feels as if it is coming from very far away
muffled by the roar of blood moving through my body
my heart's painful & urgent percussion

i begin stuffing papers back into my bag, looking
anywhere but at her. what i don't say is that i can't believe
farah of all people is using words like *reputation*

& the freedom i envied in her, that awed me in her
fades away when i look at her now, not free, but farah
small & alone, the loneliness in her painted eyes

what i do say is *thanks, i have to go, i'll see you*
next class i guess before ducking out the door
silencing that other part of me, that smallest part,
that wants to ask what she knows

SECRETS

i ride quietly back home in aunt aida's car
confused & embarrassed
but mostly disappointed in this workshop
i've looked forward to all month
becoming another secret i have to hold

but i won't look ungrateful in front of aunt aida
so when she asks, i make my voice chipper & say
it was great! i really like it
& her small smile makes the lie worth it

REPUTATION

i get home & mama is rummaging
in her purse for keys
clicking around on heeled sandals
& wearing a bright magenta tobe
her perfume oil trailing her every motion.
there's a plate for you in the microwave
she calls to me

make sure to clean up after yourself.
i'm going to some ziyaras.
aida, you haven't gone to see huda yet
& congratulate her on the new baby.
i'm going there now.
at this aunt aida catches my eye & makes
a face, coaxing an earnest & surprised laugh
from deep inside my chest
before she replies to mama

sorry, i have plans, but tell them hello from me?
& before she has even finished my mother is shaking
her head in disapproval

you know that isn't how it works. will you at least
give her a call? it's bad enough you didn't go sit
with manal for the beit bika when her father passed.
it doesn't look good at all. people will talk

& now aunt aida is rolling her eyes openly.
it doesn't look good? to who? i don't have time

for this old country social nonsense, & i honestly
don't care. huda is a smug little—
here she catches herself, remembering my presence

i leave them to their conversation & head upstairs
their voices trailing behind me as aunt aida continues
huda is a smug little . . . cow & thinks her life's great
accomplishment was getting married
& that it somehow makes her better than me.
do i make people i barely know come over
for tea every time i get a promotion?

WHAT I KNOW BY HEART

i listen for mama's & aunt aida's muffled voices
until they finally reach the front door

& as soon as i hear mama's key
in the lock, i rush for the house phone

& dial horus's number, & after two rings
his burnt-sugar voice pours sweetly
through the receiver   *hello?*

hey, it's me, this is the house phone, sorry.
are you free? i wanted to hear your voice

& within minutes i am laughing & sighing
& drinking in every note of his voice

every detail of his day
until he finally has to go

his parting words filling me with light & color
i love the sound of your voice

you should call me more often. what if we make it
our little tradition, you calling me every night?

& by the time he hangs up i miss him already
faced with the rest of the evening alone

i log on to the computer
& post a new poem to the forum:

arimasamira:

what i know by heart

my mother is my greatest love, my biggest fear

my body, the shipyard to which all my parts are tethered

my home is a place in time, is gold, is faint,

is soaked to the seams in blood

my hair is snarled, is foreign, the river i keep draining,

the plumes of smoke clinging to a recent ruin

my father is not here

my mornings are quiet, my afternoons are quiet,

my evenings full of shining teeth in laughter,

my nights the hum of a head i cannot quiet

my language is a joke i borrow to mask the clumsiness

my friends are pieces of music, are not afraid of me, show all their

teeth when they laugh, leave so much quiet when they are gone

HORUS

a few hours later the familiar envelope
starts blinking on my screen
a message from horus.
i open it, ready for the usual sweetness
the usual praise of *beautiful*
but all it says is

eyeamhorus:

i thought i told you to stop posting poems here

& i don't understand the tone
so i call him
over & over.
it rings one time then goes to voice mail.
another message appears on my screen

eyeamhorus:

i don't want to talk right now

i tried to help you

to protect you

and you don't listen to me

so we have nothing to talk about

i try again & again to call.
an hour passes, & he will not answer
hasn't sent any more messages

in a daze i call first lina, then tamadur.
they're at my door in minutes
& before they can ask about my tear-streaked face

i whimper
i think he just broke up with me

TAMADUR & LINA

tamadur hugs me while i heave out sobs
her neck & shoulder wet with my tears ·

when i finally pull away she smiles, says gently
i was starting to worry that all that water

would make my earrings turn green
& i manage a damp hiccup of a laugh

we crowd onto my bed, cross-legged
& as i tell them what happened

i notice a furrow deepening in lina's brow
though she waits until i'm done before she bursts out

he seriously said, "i thought i told you not to do that"?
what is he, your mom?

i don't like this at all, samira, & honestly, he can
stay gone & do us all a favor

i turn away from her, my face growing hot
with anger & shame

but she reaches for my hand.
wait, hey, stop, stay with me for a second.

listen, did anyone ever tell you
what really happened with farah?

& i shake my head
my anger replacing itself for a moment with curiosity

with an answer to the question
i thought we were never to ask her

FARAH

she left me a note before she moved out
lina begins

& explained everything,
told me everyone would spread

a different version of the story, but she wanted
her sister to know the truth

i don't know if you remember this,
but farah was engaged

to that guy faisal, aunt huwaida's son,
huda's cousin. & here tamadur can't help but giggle

you're like my mom, you know everyone's
entire family tree

lina rolls her eyes but smiles a little, continues
anyway, so she & faisal were engaged

& you know, she was a virgin, & his family
is like, famously strict about that stuff

they're like, display-the-sheet serious,
but he somehow sweet-talked farah into, you know,

sleeping together, before they were married,
& then like, knowing he'd locked her down

by having this secret to hold over her, he started
showing his real colors, mask off

& tamadur butts in again
i think people say "true colors"

& lina waves her hand like she's shooing a fly.
okay, whatever, his "true colors"

& just started being really shitty to her,
controlling, saying she couldn't wear this or that

or talk to so-&-so or go to the mall or use
the internet, all sorts of wild stuff

& eventually she couldn't take it anymore
& broke it off, & i swear to god

they hadn't been broken up for a full hour before
he started telling everyone that she wasn't a virgin

that she was dirty & kept trying to get him
to have sex with her, spreading rumors that she'd

lost it to some american guy.
& by the time farah tried to tell her side of the story

no one would believe her, you know,
there's no way to prove whether or not he's ever had sex

so he got to play like he was this perfect religious son
who'd been tricked by this girl

& mama & baba were so ashamed
they tried to send her back to sudan at first

to some relatives that don't really follow
everything that goes on with the community here

& she kept trying to reason with them,
& they wouldn't listen, so one day

she just took some of her clothes & her books
& she ran

RISK

we sit awhile in silence
absorbing the whole story

before i touch lina's shoulder & murmur
lina, i'm so sorry, i didn't know

i take a second to weigh out my next few words.
but also, i don't see how this relates to me & horus

we haven't had sex, i would have told you, i swear
& just as tamadur yelps a shocked *are you planning to?*

lina cuts her off, angry now.
oh my god, you're being so stupid

what i'm trying to get you to hear is that you're risking
everything to be with him, & the least he can do

on his end is be good to you! why risk everything
for someone who treats you like that?

who's controlling & ignores your calls & won't let you
post on a poetry website? seriously? it's not worth it, sam,

please listen, he's really not worth it, & you've already been
cutting it so close i'm surprised you haven't been caught

just stop while you're ahead, before your mom
decides to get really drastic & decides you can't

go to college or something like that, & dude stop shaking
your head & listen to me why won't you listen?

AUNT AIDA

in the quiet hum of aunt aida's car
she leaves me to my thoughts

we pull into the parking lot early, as usual
twenty minutes until workshop starts

samira? her voice, though quiet
jolts me from my spiral

samira, are you okay?
& i nod automatically

but something is catching in my throat
i'm fine comes out as a pitiful squeak

she sighs, twisting a ring
around her index finger

if it's stuff with your mom, just try to believe
that she means well. she's doing the best she can

& i nod again, hollowly
& when i do not answer she continues

this world she raised you in is not her world,
not the world any of us grew up in

all those rules, she's just trying to keep you safe.
& she might not even be sure from what,

but she's trying to keep you safe.
i hook a finger into the hole forming

in the thigh of my jeans.
i am safe

to which aunt aida laughs, sadly
oh, samira, the world isn't safe for any girl, honey

it's about time
you start to understand that

WORKSHOP

i spend the workshop slouched into my chair
barely registering farah's voice, which arrives
as if from very far away
carrying fragments of thought i would usually
have hurried to get down into my notebook

. . . instead of reading the poem for sense
we read it for sensation *. . .*

i hear everyone around me
scrambling to write that down

i scribble the word "sensation" onto the page
& remember horus's hand brushing mine.
i will the welling tear not to fall

now farah, in the distance, is elaborating
on another thought . . . *& maybe consonants
are percussion, & vowels are melody . . .
it matters what sounds your poems make,
what song they are trying to sing . . .*

i remember the first notes of our song
of "no ordinary love," & horus's face
approaching mine, that first kiss, the one
that might have also been our last.
the tear lands & smudges the page

HORUS

though it's only been a few weeks since
i met him

only a few weeks of horus's voice
in my ear

his messages in my inbox
his mouth on mine

without him
i am lonelier than i've ever been

everyone i know seems so far away
moving through their separate lives unhurt

& even when they try to make
contact, tamadur & lina & mama & aunt aida

everyone who loves me
it is not their love

i am aching for, & i turn away.
even the poems have dried up

have lost their electricity
without his eyes to read them

i turn in a half-hearted attempt
for workshop

& farah approaches me as i am packing up
my bag at the end of the session

*samira, i hope it isn't weird for you that i'm the one
teaching this workshop, & i can imagine the things*

*you've grown up hearing about me,
i can imagine you probably can't tell your mom*

that i'm the instructor here

here she smiles wryly.
i know more than enough about carrying a secret around

anyway, i brought some books i thought you might like.
& she tips a small pile onto the table in front of me

i sweep them into my bag without looking.
thanks i offer weakly & head out to aunt aida's car

FREEWRITE

when you are gone i spill & stay that way,
a stain, until you come back
to contain me.

i cannot be this way, a liquid girl
in love with a man made of glass.

TAMADUR & LINA

tamam_al_tamam:

sam what are the odds ur mom will let u out of the house

i'm thinking we should have some sort of rehearsal for the showcase

can u make it?

lina1234567:

miss you sam

can u let us know how ur doing?

tamam_al_tamam:

sam bb yes or no about rehearsal?

trying to figure out which day works for everyone

tamam_al_tamam:

helloooooo

earth to samira

paging samira abdullahi

?

HORUS

back at home i pass mama in the living room
watching one of her soap operas.
i offer a listless wave before shuffling to my room
& burrowing into bed
wondering how early is too early to just go
to sleep & hope tomorrow will feel better
when i hear a faint chime from my computer
the sound of a message arriving
& i rush to the desk
so full of hope it hurts my stomach
presses down onto my chest
& when i click open the envelope it's him, out of the blue
& in just a few words he's made the sun reappear
& cleared the shadows & let me back into the world

eyeamhorus:

i'm sorry. let's try again

HORUS

& now we're back as we should be
all our small traditions reinstated

every night before bed
i sneak the house phone from its cradle

& hide it in my room
wait for mama's sleeping silence across the hall

& dial his number
& it's as if i am drinking his voice

as if i am breathing it
& i always feel a little light-headed after

& i'm writing again
& i'm sending him everything

i spend my entire day waiting
for the way he says *beautiful*

the rush of my words being read
by the one they're written for

THE POEM

i've kept my promise to allow him to protect me
to protect my work

so i've stopped posting on the poetry website
i'm barely spending any time on it at all

but tonight horus is busy, a show running late
some sort of party after

tamadur & lina off having their summer
& even mama is over at aunt aida's

so i click open the window & wrap myself
in the words of others

i lose myself in an endless scroll
until i reach a video

& in its frame that face i know so well
that face i love

& it's dated a few weeks back
he hasn't told me he's been writing

i click, & the video begins to play.
the title sends a shiver of pleasure

a shiver of hope
down the length of my spine

LOVE POEM
& i know it's about me

as i grin stupidly into the screen
until the poem begins

LOVE POEM

i think i met all the

wrong ones before

you and i think they

ruined me but i

think you're really

beautiful the way

a map is beautiful,

with skin wide open

soaked in the whole

world's ink. i

think i'm done pulling

paint off the walls i

think i want to read

you the names of

every city that ever

burned down, i think

we'd like it there

& the poem is my poem
& i don't know what to do

The lord of the dark underworld, the king of the multitudinous dead, carried [Persephone] off when, enticed by the wondrous bloom of the narcissus, she strayed too far from her companions.

—EDITH HAMILTON, *MYTHOLOGY*

ALONE

i'm scrambling for the phone
dialing first tamadur & then lina
but neither will answer

i start to call aunt aida
but halfway through her number
i remember she's with mama
who can't know about any of this

i've never felt more alone
& i did it to myself

i was the one who went looking
for trouble
who left the safety
of mama's house to see
what was lurking outside
left the safety of mama's house
for a taste of red fruit

maybe everyone was always right
a bad girl, all wrong.
i'm getting exactly what i deserve
& i did it to myself

HORUS

i pass the hours in a daze
& then before i lose my nerve
i send him a message
short & sweet
just the video
& below it
did you think i wouldn't find out?

it's late
i've barely managed
to fall into a short & fitful sleep
& the phone rings
a single clear note
that jolts me awake

i've left the computer on & it chimes
as a message arrives
then another
& another
it's him

eyeamhorus:

are you there?

i didn't want to have to call your house

but i have to talk to you

hello?

& before i can decide what to do
the phone rings again
just once
i stuff it under my pillow & start typing

arimasamira:

please stop

i'm here but please stop calling

i'm going to get in so much trouble

we can talk here

THE APOLOGY

eyeamhorus:

samira, i swear i gave you credit

i said

"this is a remix of a poem by a brilliant poet, who is also my girlfriend"

i said

"it's a poem she wrote for me"

"& it meant so much to me that i had to share it with you all"

you're my muse

i thought you knew that

arimasamira:

but it doesn't say that anywhere in the video

the video is just you reading my exact poem

with like two words changed

eyeamhorus:

whoever took that video didn't start recording until after i said that i had no control over that

i would never steal from you

i actually can't believe you thought that i would steal from you

your "exact poem with like two words changed"

is that really what you think of me?

& by the end of our talk
dawn is bluing the sky outside my window
& i am the one who is apologizing

& he is wrapping me in the warm light
of his forgiveness
the word *girlfriend*
the word *muse*
draped around me like silk

HORUS

maybe because it's so late
& maybe because i'm tired

maybe because i'm terrified
of the phone ringing again
& waking mama

maybe because my anger
is an ocean between me & horus
& i miss him already on this lonely
end of the shore

maybe because he's the only one
who's ever made me feel
like a real poet
maybe because he's the only real poet
i've ever met
& his presence lights my path

maybe because of the memory
of his mouth on mine or maybe
because of the particular spark
that fuels my poems, the knowledge
that he will read each one, that each
was written for his eyes first

maybe because i don't know if
without him i'm still a poet
a tree falling alone in the forest

& no other ears around to hear me land
maybe because he feels
like my only shot at all of it
i believe him when he tells me the story
i really do believe him

FREEWRITE

NOTES FROM WORKSHOP

sensation

vowels = melody

consonants = percussion

matters what songs your poems are trying to sing

if i were your language i would make sure i was a whispered
language / a language of breath spilled like syrup from the lips
to perch in love / in confidence / onto the slope of your neck /
cupped in the dip of your ear / pooled in the hollow
of your collarbone / in love / you make music sound
like music / you make my name sound like muse / i think
before i met you i was unsung / then you arrived and with
your breath made me a language / spoke me / spoke to me /
made my name into our song / if i were your language i think
you'd learn all my secrets / like a scholar / like a scribe /
like i belonged in your breath / you make language sound
so much like music that i think you must have a song
for me / think i could be a song for you / a secret /
whispered onto the nape of your neck / safe in the dip
of your ear / pooled in the hollow of your collarbone
to call home and stay awhile / and i know languages die out
when we forget the words / don't forget me / don't leave me here
in silence

POETS

with horus back & lighting my day
i turn my attention to the abandoned pile
of books that farah lent me
& they are beautiful
their poems alive & vibrant

they feel written by people i know
people i could become.
i devour each one in a single sitting
& copy my favorite lines into a notebook

& each time i sit down to write, i read over
them to guide me, to invite their bright colors
& electric language into my brain
to brighten my own colors
electrify my own language

some of them even retell my favorite myths,
reinterpret them, complicate what i first read
as simple stories about good & evil, persephone
& hades, captor & captive & grieving mother.
they write into the long silences left by the men
who write down history, who never once
mentioned the will of the girl, caught between
man & mother

i search up the authors' names on the computer
& as their faces load onto the screen i see that many
of them are young, someone i could be in just
a handful of years, familiar shades & features
of their faces, the lilting sounds of their names

i watch videos of them reciting their work
& feel the familiar fizz of excitement once reserved
only for horus's poems.
they recite as if they are speaking directly to me
exactly to me
poems about lost homelands & lost languages
about the burden & blessing of our collectivist cultures
of belonging so hard to a people that it hurts
so hard that it leaves a mark

BOOKS

a few days later i'm back at workshop
returning the small pile of books to farah
& thanking her
& asking if she has any more

she pushes the books back toward me.
they're for you. they're yours to keep,
& next time i see them i want to see those pages
marked up. underline your favorite lines

& make notes in the margins & look up
any words you don't know, any words
you'd like to try. the book is a living thing,
& it gives back what you put into it

& i've never been allowed to write inside a book
& i think i'd like to write one of my own, someday
with wide margins for a reader's pen

GABRIEL

right before the start of workshop
a boy slides into the seat beside mine
gazes excitedly at the pile of books
on the desk before me

wow, good stack, are you reading
all these? notes from the divided country
was such a game changer for me! oh my god,
& you're reading darwish! suheir hammad!
averno is such a banger—those persephone poems?!
this whole list is like, my dream dinner party.
which poems are your favorites?

& i look up into a broad smile full of thick, even teeth
his skin clear & shining, hair lush & dark
& cut close to his head, eyes bright & alert
& rimmed with lashes thicker than my own.
hi, by the way, i'm gabriel

i am awed by his fluency, his familiarity
the way he recites lines from memory before flipping
to their exact page, the names he knows
for their devices, their forms
sestina, pantoum, double sonnet, ghazal.
i beg my brain to remember the words
too embarrassed to openly
write them down as he talks
to reveal my inexperience
my rudimentary knowledge

but he is generous with his knowing
is already scribbling things down on a torn sheet
of paper before passing it to me
a list of titles & more names
handbook of poetic forms
autobiography of red
agha shahid ali
podcasts & interview series & online journals
& i am so moved i say nothing
drinking in the spiky handwriting
on the page before me

after he finishes talking, his breathless voice slowing
to a halt, he makes sheepish eye contact, winces
his face falling.
i'm so sorry, this was probably really intense
you really don't have to humor me, i just thought—
& here i understand what he misheard inside my silence.
i put one hand on his arm
& with the other clutch his list to my heart.
no, don't you dare apologize.
this is the best thing.
you're the best.
thank you so much

FREEWRITE

1
wet, beating heart
suspended in my liquid chest

2
three days the sun seemed gone forever
i sat rumpled & coffee-stained & sad

3
a brass-colored desert body
never saved by a boy who will not swim

4
i was born at the meeting of two rivers
born where the two niles meet

5
i come from men who are gone, beautiful as falcons
gently tracing the wound of my country's broken heart

eyeamhorus:

beautiful

Samira,

Another great poem! Its scope is really impressive—it contains so much, at such a large scale, using such economy of language. The images have almost a bird's-eye view feel to them. I probably sound like a broken record at this point, but once again: this would really benefit from a proper title. Think of the title as what frames the poem, the doorway through which your reader will enter the poem. I've made some suggestions for minor line edits and marked those up directly on the poem. As always, let me know if you have any questions, or have trouble reading my handwriting (you wouldn't be the first), or would like to discuss any of these notes. Always, always a pleasure reading your work.

—Free

PS: you've got TALENT.

WORKSHOP

everyone finishes trickling into the room
& we settle into our desks as farah passes
around copies of the poems to be workshopped
mine at the very top of the pile

at first it's hard.
the only feedback i've ever gotten on any
of my writing is horus typing *beautiful*
into my inbox after each poem i send

but in here i almost can't hear the praise
over the loud siren of their critiques
a compliment about my imagery muffled
by a note that the poem feels *a little scattered*

something nice about my use of verbs
forgotten as soon as i hear *just a list of pretty images*
with nothing really collecting them into a poem
& for the fifteen minutes i'm being workshopped

i feel myself on the edge of tears
busying myself writing everything down so no one
will see my face
& just as the first drop lands onto my open notebook
gabriel's voice pipes up to my left

i actually don't agree with that critique at all.
i think the title does all the work of collecting
those images under a sort of umbrella,

& actually i think it's unfair to read the work
through the lens of what you think
a poem is supposed *to be instead of reading it*
for the poem it already is, you know what i mean?
& i feel myself unshrinking

as the rest of the group shuffles their papers to the next poem
i tear a corner of a page from my notebook
& write *thank you* in a hurried scrawl
before passing it to him

GABRIEL

crouched in the hallway
stuffing the pages covered with notes
into my bag, ready to escape to aunt aida's
waiting car, i see gabriel approach, almost
as if he'd been looking for me

i actually saw you read at the open mic
the other week. you were really good

he falls into easy step beside me toward the exit
as we climb together onto that particular giddy cloud
of new friendship

we are already making plans to write together
to go to another open mic

but as he takes out his phone i interrupt
& his smile wilts a little

i don't have my phone right now,
i'm grounded, it's a long & really stupid story,
but anyway, yeah, no phone these days, but i can
still message online, from the computer

& his smile is back & cloudless
yeah, that works, let's do that
just as we reach the parking lot

i turn to him & wave before clambering into the car
where aunt aida's expressive left eyebrow is arched
into a question

he's in my workshop, i just met him today
i start to explain

& she waves my story off with a laugh.
don't worry, you don't need to lawyer up,
i think it's great that you're meeting other poets

gabrielthepoet:

your poems are really amazing

it's so interesting what ur doing with form

those lists of images that kind of accumulate

it's so cool

xo_samira_07:

ahaha thank you :) :)

gabrielthepoet:

who are some of ur influences?

xo_samira_07:

idk really

i love reading the poems on this online forum

and i'm getting into like greek mythology

but idk

my favorite poet is horus though

do u know his work?

gabrielthepoet:

i've heard of him yeah

maybe i should take another look at his work

the stuff i've seen never really grabbed me

not bc it isn't good but bc it's kind of all over the place

like every poem seems written by a different poet kinda

like idk that i could point out

what makes a poem of his feel like a poem of his

but your work for example

i've only seen a few poems

but now i feel like i'd recognize a poem of urs from a mile away

RE:

From: Tamadur Ibrahim <tamadur.ibra@whs.edu>
To: Samira Abdullahi <samira.abdul@whs.edu>; Mazin Hamid
<mazin.hamid@whs.edu>; Hamza Sharif <h.sharif@whs.edu>;
Wiaam Sharif <wshar@email.com>; Azza Aziz
<aaziz@cdhs.edu>; Ola Salih <osalih@cdhs.edu>
Subject: the big night!

hello sweet people! we have a venue (16th st community center!)
we have a date (saturday august 1!) we have a call time (5:30 pm!)
and we have a showtime (7-9 pm!)

sam, mazin, azza, ola, you'll each get 10-15 min to do ur thing! i'll
get back to u soon with an order! & then there's a dance troupe
that's gonna do some stuff in between ur sets!

& wiaam, let me know if just a regular folding table works for u or
if you'll need any sort of special setup!

hamza, let me know if you can meet me at the venue a few hours
before so we can get those paintings up!

ok sorry for all the exclamation marks i just am thrilled i hope ur
thrilled i can't wait!!!!!!!

thank u all for saying yes xoxoxoxoxo

PERSEPHONE

call a myth what it is:
the surviving whispers of history

its long generations of aunts
& poets

i heard,
it first began

winged & feathered,
flitting

from mouth to mouth,
reshaped at each turn

until nobody can remember
how it started:

i heard she was taken
/
i heard she went willingly

even her name trickles like water
into new shapes

persephone
/
prosperine

i heard she wanted to stay gone
/
i heard she missed her mother

i heard a whole world went hungry
in the name of one matriarch's grief

melinoia
/
melindia

even on the matter
of what to call her

the stories
do not agree:

daughter of demeter
/
onlyborn of ceres

beloved of hades
/
pluto's captive wife

the only fact that remains consistent
is that she ate the fruit

this girl with a thousand names
with none

with bright red
on her hands, in her mouth:

it was seven seeds
/
it was four of them

some say it was only one
& that was all it took to ruin her

in the version of the story
i've been told

she was tainted by the fruit
sentenced forever

to spend a season
in the lower world:

some say half the year
/
some say a few months

but what if it freed her
from that other tyranny

the mother's hand clamped tight
around her arm, until it bruised

until it bloomed bright
as pomegranates

the story leaves gaps
wide enough to whisper into

wide enough to see
my own name

WRITING PROMPT

we've been sent home from workshop
with the assignment to read the work
of a poet named ai
no last name
just that tiny cluster of vowels
& some notes from farah
on something she calls *persona*
a poem written in the voice
of someone else

& i know right away whose voice i choose
the one i've secretly been writing poems with
for years to fill the quiet where her actual voice
so rarely addresses me

i title it "portrait of my mother at my age"
& for the ending stanza i borrow some lines
from ai, from a poem of hers that thrilled me
like a movie would, its last sentences so strange
& menacing & sad
i can break your heart

mazinha:

tamadur are you inviting parents to ur showcase thing

i wanna bring amber

but i don't want to deal w my dad

o.la.la.la:

lol at amber coming to this sudani event

are you gonna dress her up in a little tobe and everything

hamzapaints:

what happened to the group text

i can't keep up with all these different platforms

lina1234567:

samira's grounded and doesn't have her phone

tamam_al_tamam:

yes it's called being *inclusive*

azzabackwardsisazza:

lol hamza don't act like you mind

we can all see you liking every one of tamadur's pictures

like .5 seconds after she posts

iamwiaam:

ooh yikes hamza that's not a good look lil brother

tam is like our distant cousin

why don't u try dating outside the family

GABRIEL

when mama leaves for work
i catch the bus to meet gabriel at the café
that usually hosts the open mic, though it's still
early in the day, & we're meeting to work
on the prompt for workshop
& i can't wait to show him what i wrote

when i arrive i am glazed in sweat
from the humid summer afternoon
& find him spotless in a white t-shirt
at a low table surrounded by soft chairs
a half-drained black coffee in a chipped mug
in front of him as he smiles up at me

how are you drinking hot coffee in this weather?
i groan, trying to discreetly air out my armpits
plucking at the fabric of my shirt, dark with sweat
& he grins. *hot drinks actually help cool you down,*
did you know? i eye him suspiciously

you sound like my mom i say, rolling my eyes
she loves drinking tea, like in the middle of a ninety-degree
afternoon, & i'm sorry but it sounds made up
& the laugh sings out of him, a warm & clear note
as i sink into a chair beside him

A POET

for the first hour it's like we both
forget we're here to work
our conversation unspooling
in a thousand directions
jokes & stories & our favorite songs
the earnest way he talks about his favorite books
quoting whole passages from memory

& it would normally make me shy
talking to someone who knows something
i don't, but his tone is open & invites me in
invites my questions & listens seriously
when i talk about my poems, about that feeling
i am chasing, trying to get close to that perfect
poem that lives only in my head, that i am trying
to inch my way toward

& he nods, excitement beaming from him like heat
exactly, i know exactly what you mean,
the way you put it is so perfect
& when asked how he came to know
so much about books, about poems
he tells me about his dad, the professor, the celebrated
writer, a continent away, who sees his son so rarely
that he doesn't realize how much he was made
in his image, a poet in his own right

BORROWING

i read my poem for workshop aloud to gabriel
relishing the ending lines i borrowed from ai
& when i look up, expecting his open & easy smile
i see a furrow in his brow

can i see what it looks like on the page? he asks
& i nod, suddenly nervous, & pass him my notebook

he scans it quickly, his eyes moving across the page
the furrow deepening in his brow, & for a while
he chews on his lip as i watch him measure out
his words

samira, this is really great, really beautiful,
but—& i hope i'm not making this weird,
but that last stanza—i don't know how to say
this really, it's not an accusation, but i think
those lines are exactly the same as in the poem
by ai that we looked at in workshop

& the relief loosens my tensed muscles
oh my god, is that why you look so stressed out?
no, totally, they are ai's lines, i just borrowed them
because i thought it would be a cool ending
for my poem! sort of like a remix, i add
remembering my conversation with horus

& gabriel looks uncomfortable again
but is softer this time.

okay, i hear you, & i really loved
those lines too, but when you have them
on the page like that, no italics or quotation marks
or footnotes or anything, it makes it look like
the lines are supposed to be yours,
you know? & you can get in a lot of trouble
for that, as a poet, for plagiarism, it's really hard
to come back from something like that

& the word *plagiarism* hits my brain
in a shower of hot colors

HORUS

i float home in a haze of distraction, the word
plagiarism crowding my brain. the house is empty,
silent, mama still not home from work
& my thoughts are so loud i barely register my legs
moving as i climb the stairs to my room
where i sit immediately at the computer
to two new messages

i go to open gabriel's first

gabrielthepoet:

let me know if you wanna talk more about that remix thing

and even if u don't feel comfortable talking to me about it

maybe u could talk to free?

then feel immediately guilty
for choosing him, feeling like
i've somehow betrayed horus
so instead of answering i exit
& click open the envelope from horus.
my eyes scan the quick lines

eyeamhorus:

hey beautiful girl

i'm in your city tomorrow

can i see you?

& i push the earlier word from my mind.
i'll just ask him, & he'll have another
explanation, & gabriel is just a kid while horus
is a real poet whose words carry him around
the country, around the world.
i tell myself i'll talk to him, but i feel myself
already believing whatever it is he'll say
so i simply type back

arimasamira:

yes

lina1234567:

after my game tomorrow can we go to the mall

i need a new swimsuit

i think i'm officially a full b cup now

tamam_al_tamam:

ugh not fairrrr

share the wealth!!!!!

but yes good plan

xo_samira_07:

i don't think i can come out tomorrow :(

don't wanna risk it w mama

sorry :(:(:(

tamam_al_tamam:

rare samira sighting in the inbox!!!!

where have u been we miss you

SURVEILLANCE

once again i measure out the time
i have between mama's exit

in the morning for work
& her return in the early evening

those precious eight hours mine
to fill with horus

with his smell & his touch
& memories to tide me over

until our next meeting.
i shake my hair out into its full power

i douse myself freely with mama's perfume oil
i start applying my favorite red lipstick

then worry it will discourage him from kissing me
so i blot it all off with some tissue

i board the bus & slink into a seat in the back
my face partially hidden inside a book just in case

& in my descent into the dark mouth
of the metro station

i scan the surrounding escalators for any familiar
set of eyes, any familiar headscarf

& when i reach my stop the steady glide
of the escalator takes me up

toward a sky blazing blue
toward horus

smiling at me & dappled
in the late-morning sun

HORUS

he meets me at the top of the escalator
picks me up & spins me & wraps me in his scent
the velvet of his mouth on mine
murmurs into my ear
i'm obsessed with the way you smell

& in that moment i feel exactly as he sees me
elegant & grown-up & free
not the cloistered daughter
not the shameful girl.
today i belong not to the stares
& whispers of the aunties
not to my mother's iron grip
but to him

the hard musculature of his chest
tight coils of his hair
& the freedom slants into me like a drug
& unlatches me from my fear
from my shame
as we walk together down u street
his shoulder grazing my shoulder

i reach for his hand
& hold it triumphantly in mine

HORUS

he is beside me
he is real

the weeks of messages
& phone calls

collecting into his scent & solid form
his readily available touch

& i begin to imagine
the life we could spend together

we duck into a small shop
scented with incense

where he promptly adorns himself
with three enormous rings

inlaid with complicated-looking patterns
of stones, holds up a pair of heavy brass earrings

& announces that they were made for me
& that he can no longer deprive himself

of the sight of them against what he calls
my *pharaonic neck*

buys them for me, & as we exit the shop,
i feel their weight in my ears

& as his fingers lace tightly around mine
i feel the shape of his new rings pressing into my skin

& i am stunned at my own happiness
at our bodies

in step together & gleaming
in the sunlight

TRANSFORMATION

against the golden hour as the sun begins to dip
into its escape toward night

i part reluctantly with horus at union station
replaying that last kiss until i'm giddy

& almost miss my stop on the way home
& once i'm home i go through the same practiced motions

of making myself look like this day didn't happen
a shower to wash away the perfume, the makeup

sweatpants & my hair tamed back into a single braid.
in the mirror i try to conjure the memory of that other girl

i was today—cat-eyed & kissed & glossy in the sun
wandering the summertime city, hand in hand
with my boyfriend, my fellow poet, grown-up & in love—
but i can't find her face in the soft, scrubbed roundness of mine

TAMADUR & LINA

as the sun sets
i settle at the computer
& scan the screen for a message
from horus, but he hasn't sent one yet.
instead i see a series of messages
from tamadur, in all caps:

tamam_al_tamam:

EXCUSE ME HI

WE MISS YOU

(LINA IS HERE TOO)

*CAN WE HIJACK ANOTHER MOTHER-DAUGHTER
DINNER OR SOMETHING*

CAN'T BEAR ANOTHER DAY W/O UR FACE!!!!!

laughing to myself i rise to fetch the house phone
& within the hour we are together again
piled onto the couch

our laughter so contagious that even mama
coming home from work to find us
can't help a small smile of her own

TAMADUR & LINA

i hadn't let myself feel how much
i was missing them

& hadn't let myself admit
i'd been sort of avoiding them

since we last saw each other
when horus & i were fighting

when it felt like i had to choose
& i won't make that choice

i want all my loves around me
even if i have to keep them separate

even if i have to keep it to myself
that i've reunited with horus

i'll keep it
just one more sentence

in my lifelong language of silence
though in all the years

that tam & lina & i have been friends
it's the first time i've kept something from them

but i'll keep it
so i can keep them

so i can keep him.
i've trained all my life for this secret

MAMA

i part with tamadur & lina for the night
with hugs & their promises to come back soon

their presence was a balm
a brightness

mama still wears that small smile
& hums to herself

as she washes the dinner dishes
without summoning me to help

i hover awkwardly by the kitchen door
unsure if i should interrupt her moment

to resume my usual chore at the sink.
she looks up as if she can sense my hesitation

& her face softens.
why don't you make us some tea while i finish these?

& maybe we can watch a movie,
if you'd like?

& i hadn't realized until just now
how much i've missed her

MAMA

the tea wafts little notes of cardamom, of clove
& something black & white is playing on the screen

as mama sinks back into the cushions of the couch
with a sigh, takes a practiced sip of scalding tea

while i stir heaping spoonfuls of sugar into my cup.
i feel guilty for the part of me that wants to pretend

to get something from my room, or use the bathroom
so i can check the computer for a message from horus

but i tell myself i'll be quick, that it'll only take a second
but as i start setting the sugar spoon down onto the tray

mama begins, dreamily, to speak.
your grandfather loved poetry, did i ever tell you?

he would have loved to know you. i wish you could
have seen the old house, he had a room for just his books,

shelves from floor to ceiling, never dusty because
he was always reaching for one or the other, to read

aloud to someone, to look something up. i hope
there's an eternity of books for him now,

wherever he's gone to rest.
here she goes silent for a while

& i don't know if i'm meant to say something
so i murmur *allah yirhamu*

as i settle back into my seat
accepting that it might be some time

until i can head back to the computer. she never
really talks about her life before, mama, she never

really tells me anything about what & who she's lost
so i start to ask her questions, & the night unfurls

its hours until it is probably past midnight, & still
we sit together, the teacups drained & heaps

of discarded pistachio shells scattered on the table before us
as she tells me about her girlhood, her dreams

of being a professor. *of what?* i ask
& she shakes her head, smiling. *of anything,*

i just wanted the white tobe, the elegance,
the chalk dust on my hands, a desk messy with books & papers

& you know, my father supported it, gave me permission
to go away to university in cairo. your aunt aida

was already studying in london by then. but then your father
asked for my hand right before i was set to go, &

my path changed. here she trails off, & i feel
like i should apologize, so i do, & the softness

comes back into her face as she takes both my hands in hers.
samira, no, don't misunderstand. i'm not sorry at all,

& i would do it again, & again, because this path
gave me my beautiful, brilliant daughter. you'll be the one

who goes away for university, who makes all of us proud.
& i work to silence the guilt gnawing at my stomach

MAMA

yawning, she rises
looks down at the dishes
& pistachio shells
looks over conspiratorially
& whispers
we can do those in the morning
& before the surprised smile
can fully spread across my face
i hear it
& i know even before i really know
that the moment is broken
as the house phone trills its distant ring.
mama glances at its empty cradle
murmuring to herself
who could be calling at this hour?
follows the sound upstairs to my room.
i trail her silently
blood roaring in my ears
not even trying to find a way
to get to it before her as she answers
& through the muffled receiver
i hear his voice

HORUS

my mother's voice rises to a pitch
that could break glass

who are you?

what business do you have with my daughter
at this hour?

no, that can't be true

my daughter has no boyfriend

no, you cannot speak to her

don't you dare call this number again

& as she hangs up the call she turns to look at me
& i wish her face wore anger

i wish she was seething, frothing with rage
i wish she'd scream at me & call me every name

i already have for myself, i wish she'd hurl
the receiver to the ground, or at the wall, or at me

but it's the betrayal in her face that i can't stand
the way she looks at me like she doesn't know who i am

HORUS

i was already grounded so i don't even know
what to call this

the way mama walked out of my room
& into hers, the door shutting quietly
behind her

the way i stood frozen to the spot, i don't know
for how long, before leaping to the computer
to check his messages

eyeamhorus:

loved seeing you today, beautiful girl (6:32 pm)

just got home, you awake? (10:20 pm)

hello? (10:45 pm)

lol, is it past ur bedtime? (10:51 pm)

wait, are you ignoring me? (11:05 pm)

is something wrong? (11:06 pm)

i came all the way from new york to see you (11:07 pm)

& this is the thanks i get? (11:07 pm)

nah, this doesn't work for me (11:08 pm)

you don't ignore me (11:08 pm)

samira? baby? (11:08 pm)

fine (11:10 pm)

we need to talk (1:00 am)

pick up. (1:03 am)

in the morning the computer is gone

4

Unlike the rest of us, she doesn't know
What winter is, only that she is what causes it.

—LOUISE GLÜCK, "PERSEPHONE THE WANDERER"

WHAT I'M NOT ALLOWED TO DO

stay at home alone

leave the house without mama or aunt aida

watch television

go to workshop

sit on the stoop

use any phone

use any computer

see lina

see tamadur

see anyone except mama & aunt aida

& mama has disconnected the landline

at night i still hear its phantom ring

AUNT AIDA

since i'm not allowed to be home alone
mama tried at first to bring me with her
to the office where she works as a receptionist
but i was always in the way

her desk, already small, the single chair
on its creaking wheels, the apology
in her voice at her boss's glare in my direction

so now i spend my days in aunt aida's
sharply air-conditioned office, sprawled out
on the leather sofa with a book while she types
a rapid percussion of words, talks in a clipped voice
into the forever-ringing phone, empties & refills
the same mug, eternal lipstick print on its rim

twice a day she runs to a meeting
calling over her shoulder
be back soon. don't use the computer! love you
the click of her heels echoing
down the hallway behind her

RE:

so, of course, while aunt aida's gone
i use her computer

From: Samira Abdullahi <samira.abdul@whs.edu>
To: Horus EyeAm <eye.am.horus@email.com>
Subject: (no subject)

hi i'm so sorry for disappearing my mom took away my computer
i'm writing to you now from my aunt's office

- -

From: Farah Abdelmounim <free.poetry@email.com>
To: Samira Abdullahi <samira.abdul@whs.edu>
Subject: you okay?

Hey Samira,

You weren't at workshop today—is everything okay?

Hoping all is well,
Free

Farah "Free" Abdelmounim
Teaching Artist, Teen Poetry Workshop
Wednesday Open Mic Host, Bookshelf & Mocha
Poet & Performer

From: Tamadur Ibrahim <tamadur.ibra@whs.edu>
To: Samira Abdullahi <samira.abdul@whs.edu>
CC: Lina Abdelmounim <lina.abdelmo@whs.edu>
Subject: idk how you're even checking email but idk what else
to do

sam my mom just told me what happened with ur mom (she heard
from lina's mom) how bad is it? we tried calling your house but the
number is disconnected & idk if it's ok to try coming over???

From: Samira Abdullahi <samira.abdul@whs.edu>
To: Tamadur Ibrahim <tamadur.ibra@whs.edu>
CC: Lina Abdelmounim <lina.abdelmo@whs.edu>
Subject: Re: idk how you're even checking email but idk what
else to do

i've never been in trouble like this before idk what she's going to do

---

From: Lina Abdelmounim <lina.abdelmo@whs.edu>
To: Samira Abdullahi <samira.abdul@whs.edu>
CC: Tamadur Ibrahim <tamadur.ibra@whs.edu>
Subject: Re: idk how you're even checking email but idk what
else to do

is it true he called the house phone in the middle of the night?
are you ok? i'm sorry ur locked down like this but i hope at least

it's keeping his creepy ass far away from you. i can't believe he'd
do something like that???

sorry sorry i'm just so worried for you i miss you

PS: i got an email from farah she's trying to get in touch with you
have you heard from her?

PPS: not to kick you while ur down but thanks for telling me she
was ur POETRY TEACHER???

From: Samira Abdullahi <samira.abdul@whs.edu>
To: Farah Abdelmounim <free.poetry@email.com>
Subject: Re: you okay?

hi farah i'm sorry for missing workshop i got in big trouble with
my mom and now i'm grounded
she took my computer too so i'm emailing you from my aunt's
office

From: Gabriel Diop <gdiop@cdhs.edu>
To: Samira Abdullahi <samira.abdul@whs.edu>
Subject: checking in

hey you didn't come to workshop are you good? just checking in

From: Samira Abdullahi <samira.abdul@whs.edu>
To: Gabriel Diop <gdiop@cdhs.edu>
Subject: Re: checking in

i'm grounded :(

From: Gabriel Diop <gdiop@cdhs.edu>
To: Samira Abdullahi <samira.abdul@whs.edu>
Subject: Re: checking in

that sucks i'm sorry
i can drop some books off for you in the coming days if you
want? and i'm attaching all the readings and stuff from workshop
this week. there's a prompt too. can i send you my poem when i'm
done? it's a little rough and needs work before i can turn it in to
the whole group

From: Farah Abdelmounim <free.poetry@email.com>
To: Samira Abdullahi <samira.abdul@whs.edu>
Subject: Re: you okay?

Samira,

Are you safe?

Farah

Farah "Free" Abdelmounim
Teaching Artist, Teen Poetry Workshop
Wednesday Open Mic Host, Bookshelf & Mocha
Poet & Performer

- -

From: Samira Abdullahi <samira.abdul@whs.edu>
To: Farah Abdelmounim <free.poetry@email.com>
Subject: Re: you okay?

i'm okay i think she just needs time to cool down. but i don't think i can go to workshop anymore

From: Samira Abdullahi <samira.abdul@whs.edu>
To: Gabriel Diop <gdiop@cdhs.edu>
Subject: Re: checking in

lol ur SO kind for the book thing but if my mom sees a boy
anywhere near the house she's literally gonna send me back to
sudan. send me ur poem though!

- -

From: Farah Abdelmounim <free.poetry@email.com>
To: Samira Abdullahi <samira.abdul@whs.edu>
Subject: Re: you okay?

Samira,

Do you need someone to talk to? Do you need someone to come get you?

If you still want to come to workshop, there will always be a place for you here. You're an incredibly gifted writer, and we'll all miss your words in the room. Is there anything I can do?

———

Farah "Free" Abdelmounim
Teaching Artist, Teen Poetry Workshop
Wednesday Open Mic Host, Bookshelf & Mocha
Poet & Performer

From: Samira Abdullahi <samira.abdul@whs.edu>
To: Horus EyeAm <eye.am.horus@email.com>
Subject: ???

are u getting my messages?

From: Samira Abdullahi <samira.abdul@whs.edu>
To: Farah Abdelmounim <free.poetry@email.com>
Subject: Re: you okay?

i really miss workshop and i don't know how i'm going to get out
of this mess

From: Farah Abdelmounim <free.poetry@email.com>
To: Samira Abdullahi <samira.abdul@whs.edu>
Subject: Re: you okay?

Let me see what I can do.

_____

sent on the go

- -

From: Samira Abdullahi <samira.abdul@whs.edu>
To: Horus EyeAm <eye.am.horus@email.com>
Subject: please

please say something

HORUS

for days i report to aunt aida's office
tearing through my stack of library books
making half-hearted attempts at the workshop prompts
sending a flurry of emails back & forth
with lina & tam, with gabriel
& horus does not answer my messages
& then he does

just as i am about to log off aunt aida's computer
my eye on the clock, ten minutes until she returns

- -

From: Horus EyeAm <eye.am.horus@email.com>
To: Samira Abdullahi <samira.abdul@whs.edu>
Subject: dc

i have a show in your city in a couple weeks. august 1st. it's a
saturday. can i see you?

- -

From: Samira Abdullahi <samira.abdul@whs.edu>
To: Horus EyeAm <eye.am.horus@email.com>
Subject: Re: dc

idk i want to see you but i'm so so so grounded like you wouldn't
even believe

From: Horus EyeAm <eye.am.horus@email.com>
To: Samira Abdullahi <samira.abdul@whs.edu>
Subject: Re: dc

i was really hoping i'd get to see you. i'm giving you so much advance notice. can you try?

From: Samira Abdullahi <samira.abdul@whs.edu>
To: Horus EyeAm <eye.am.horus@email.com>
Subject: Re: dc

you don't understand the only reason i can even email you rn is because my mom has me spending all day at my aunt's office where someone can keep an eye on me

---

From: Horus EyeAm <eye.am.horus@email.com>
To: Samira Abdullahi <samira.abdul@whs.edu>
Subject: Re: dc

"grounded" lol

From: Horus EyeAm <eye.am.horus@email.com>
To: Samira Abdullahi <samira.abdul@whs.edu>
Subject: Re: dc

you're too mature for that. just talk to ur mom or something

From: Samira Abdullahi <samira.abdul@whs.edu>
To: Horus EyeAm <eye.am.horus@email.com>
Subject: Re: dc

she won't even look at me and idk how bad this even is but everything is on the line for me right now, like i'm not allowed to go to workshop, i'm probably not even allowed to go away for college anymore, so there's no way she's gonna let me go to an open mic or whatever

---

From: Horus EyeAm <eye.am.horus@email.com>
To: Samira Abdullahi <samira.abdul@whs.edu>
Subject: Re: dc

"an open mic or whatever"

why do you talk to me like that?

just say you don't care enough to show up

see you around i guess

From: Samira Abdullahi <samira.abdul@whs.edu>
To: Horus EyeAm <eye.am.horus@email.com>
Subject: Re: dc

no no no that's not what i meant at all! but literally my mom
won't look at me or talk to me or let me out of the house without
her or my aunt

From: Horus EyeAm <eye.am.horus@email.com>
To: Samira Abdullahi <samira.abdul@whs.edu>
Subject: Re: dc

stop acting like ur not grown

just stand up to your mom and you'll realize that she can't
actually keep you from doing anything

grow up and stand up for yourself

anyway i'm done dealing with this over email. give me a call
whenever you actually wanna talk

blinking away tears, i turn to look at aunt aida's office phone

& before i can reach for it, before i think

to click out of the window with all the messages

i hear the door open

& the familiar sound of aunt aida's shoes

AUNT AIDA

i start to rise from her desk chair
& she motions me back down
while she sinks onto the leather couch
& slips her feet out of their shoes

working a knuckle into her arches
eyes closed, she is silent
& looks more tired than i've ever seen her

i begin before i even have the lie ready
anything to break the heavy silence
but before i even finish saying her name
she raises a hand, & the sounds wilt in my mouth

sliding each shoe back on, she finally opens
her eyes & faces me

samira, i don't know if you understand this,
but i am fighting very hard for you behind
the scenes. & i'm happy to do it, of course,

but you can't keep undoing all my work—
i don't know how much you're keeping up,
but mazin, the arabic teacher's kid?

his parents aren't letting him finish high school
here. something about a girlfriend, an american girl.
it's the oldest trick our community has:

they pretended to be going back home
for a visit, & on their last day let mazin know
that they wouldn't be returning here

& now your mother is getting ideas. we made
a plan, you & i, samira. college, new york,
all of it—i need you to start taking it seriously

& whoever he is, he isn't a degree. he isn't
your life. he isn't a path to follow, you understand?
i'm doing everything i can,

but you need to take this seriously

DOOR

in the car she acts like everything
is back to normal between us

her chatter one-sided as i stare shallowly
out the window

her voice far away behind the wall i've built.
i let myself indulge my cruelest thought:

aunt aida wouldn't understand about love
because in the sixteen years i've known her

she's always been alone
though of course i know better than to say it

the car glides onto our block, & i scramble out
mumbling my thanks

shutting the door in the middle of her promise
to pick me up in the morning

at home i don't even bother saying hello to mama
who still is not speaking to me

i pull myself up the stairs, ready for refuge
in my room with a book

& just as i think the indignities might finally
have exhausted themselves

i reach my room to find the door taken clean
off its hinges

my room framed
in the open arch left behind

HORUS

the next morning at aunt aida's office
i tell myself i will only use the computer
for five minutes & then i'll respect
aunt aida's wishes, prove to her
i'm taking her help seriously

& if she asks i'll tell a version of the truth:
that i was checking my school email

as the window loads my stomach fills
with a bright pang of excitement
at the sight of a new message with his name

- -

From: Horus EyeAm <eye.am.horus@email.com>
To: Samira Abdullahi <samira.abdul@whs.edu>
Subject: (no subject)

sorry about having an attitude yesterday. i just miss you.

hey, about the show, i think you should open for me. 7 minute set.
are u down?

say yes

i keep my promise
i send him a quick *omg yes*
& click out of the computer

& when aunt aida returns two minutes later
i am curled safely on the couch, flipping furiously
through my notebook, dreaming up a set list
for my first real show

THE VISIT

that evening as we pull up in aunt aida's car
there's another car, small & blue, parked
in front of the house

i look to aunt aida, a question in my eyes
& she shrugs. *no idea. she hasn't exactly been
in the entertaining mood*

but instead of dropping me off & continuing
into her driveway as she usually does
tonight she parks behind the blue car
& walks out with me

in the living room i see mama sitting rigid
on the couch, her mouth set in a line that means
she is either furious or she is trying not to cry

& on the other end of the couch, talking urgently
& clearly in the middle of a monologue
is farah

FARAH

she's made an effort in the way she's dressed
to endear herself to mama, i can tell: her skirt
is long & loose, & though it's hot she's draped
a scarf around her shoulders

her face is scrubbed clean of any makeup
& like this she looks younger, more vulnerable
like a girl i could know, like a girl i've been

FARAH

aunt aida & i stand unmoving in the doorway.
i clasp her hand & murmur
she's the one who teaches the poetry workshop.
i know i should have told you, but i didn't want
there to be any reason i couldn't go, it means
so much to me, i didn't know if you'd still
think it was okay.
aunt aida squeezes my hand
keeping it in hers as she steps into the room
whispering to me
i think i should stay

REMARKABLE

i trail behind as aunt aida strides purposefully
into the room, walks up to farah with her hand
extended, as if undaunted by the tension palpable
in the air. *i'm aida, samira's aunt*

then she turns to my mother. a look passes
between them that i can't understand, their own
ancient language. i see it, that ripple, older
than any sound. aunt aida lowers herself into
a chair, motions for me to take the remaining one
beside her, & when i'm seated she turns her eyes
back to farah. *i think i might have interrupted you,*
forgive me. you were saying?

& then farah is speaking again, & she is speaking
about my work, about my poems, & i understand
what it must feel like to have leaves made green
by light & water. she says *remarkable,* says *special,*
says *never before in my life, let alone my years as a teacher.*
a young poet you meet once in a lifetime, if you're lucky

& i believe her. i believe horus too, when he calls
my poems *beautiful,* but he never says much else
never says anything about them being special. has never
said *remarkable.* & then the faraway thought i try not
to indulge, that horus might not have ever cared
about my poems if he didn't also like the way i look

& maybe it's okay? i want him to find me beautiful
love to be looked at by him, the way he murmurs
beautiful, pulls me close & inhales. but i did not make
my face, my hair, the borrowed perfume oil.
& farah's praise is for what i've made, calls *spectacular*
what i can credit wholly to my own brain, my two hands

SILENCE

please.
farah looks into my mother's face
& will not look away.
please, let samira
come back to workshop.
i promise to do my best
to help keep her safe

the silence is enormous as we wait
for my mother to answer. it trickles
into everything, tightens its hold
around my throat, summons tears
into my eyes & readies them for the fall

aunt aida leans forward in her chair
opens her mouth to speak, but before
she can make a sound my mother gives
the slightest shake of her head, her mouth
still in its same hard line, & aunt aida
settles back into quiet

ASK

my mother turns & addresses me directly
for the first time in days

samira
her voice sounds exhausted, a little hoarse

you might not understand it now,
but these rules are for your sake, not mine

i'm trying to keep you safe
in this country where the culture is not our culture

& the dangers are new dangers.
i am trying to keep you safe in a country i barely understand

that voice on the phone, that was an adult man.
it's not just wearing shorts or staying out too late anymore

& a man that age, calling a girl your age, at that hour?
i don't have to know much more to know you're not safe

you are actively putting yourself in harm's way,
& i feel like i could lose you at any second

if it feels like my grip is too tight, that's why.
with every year that passes i feel you slipping

through my fingers, & you're all i have,
& i know that doesn't make me popular with you

but it's all for your sake, & i can only hope
that when you're older you'll realize that

until then, my only choice is to keep you here,
where i can keep an eye on you,

where i can keep you safe, until i can trust
that you have the judgment to do it yourself

but i haven't seen that from you yet.
in fact, i've seen the opposite

samira, the fact is that i no longer trust you.
i don't recognize the person you've become

& it feels like i haven't looked straight into her face
in years. the eyes are tired, their slight downturn

making her look always a little sad, even when she is laughing
though i can't remember the last time i even heard her laugh

& i miss her. i miss being her girl. i miss her protection,
our uncomplicated love. my grief is for that loss.

then why don't you ever ask me? i find myself blurting out.
you say you don't know me, you don't recognize me,

but i'm right here, you can ask me, you could know me
if you really wanted. but it's like you decided i don't

belong to you anymore, like you were so ashamed of me
that it was easier to pretend i wasn't yours. & all i ever want

is for you to be on my side. all those years when everyone
was gossiping about me, you always went straight into acting

like everything they said was true. so whatever i did after that,
it didn't matter, you & everyone else had already made up your minds

about me. so maybe i decided to prove you all right. because
you never asked me. you never defended me. someone said,

with no proof, that i was bad, a bad girl, & you just believe them?
you never say "don't talk about my daughter like that"

or "i'm sure she has an explanation" or "why don't you mind
your own business & let me & my daughter mind ours?"

you left me all alone, mama, when everyone was talking about me,
& you didn't say anything, you didn't do anything but add yourself

to the list of people who think there's something wrong with me.
& i just wish i had you, just you, on my side

MAMA

my mother's jaw is set, so tight it looks
almost painful, & i think she must be furious
at me for disrespecting her in front of company

but when her chin gives the slightest tremble
i understand: she is trying to keep in the tears

i'm sorry, she murmurs, so softly i almost
don't hear her at first. *i miss you too, & i'm sorry,
& i am always on your side, always. i'm sorry
i haven't been better at showing that, at acting like it*

*i will meet you in the middle if you will meet me:
i will relax my rules, but you need to stop lying
to me. you have to stop keeping secrets.
i can't help you if you don't tell me what's going on*

i'm sorry too i hiccup, my tears making every word
emerge in a wail. *i'm sorry for keeping secrets,
for not giving you a chance to understand*

she rises from her seat & envelops me in that familiar
scent, the cotton of her jalabiya washed & rewashed
for years, its decades of soap mingling with her perfume oil.
*you're my girl, my daughter, my only. all i have in this world
that matters is you. i'm sorry we got so far away*

HOME

in the days that follow, my mother & i bask

in our return to each other, watching old movies,

brewing fragrant pots of tea, playing her favorite

old songs as we bustle around the house, our voices

harmonizing out of tune. one evening she brings home

living flowers in a clay pot, sings to them in the mornings

as she checks the dampness of the soil with her fingers.

under her care they bloom into perfume & color, & so do i.

i tell her about my poems & she hugs me, talks at length about

the grandfather i never knew, asks me to consider showing

her the poems, only when i feel ready. it's as if i've stumbled

on that sweeter past version of us, the way she loved me

when i was little, now restored, her hands applying karkaar

to my hair, a little vial of her perfume oil left for me

in my room

HOME ALONE

a week later, as if to prove her trust in me
mama leaves me home alone for an entire weekend
aunt aida her reluctant companion
on a trip to michigan for a distant relative's wedding

TAMADUR & LINA

TAMADUR:

lina can i ride to michigan with u and ur mom

i won't survive that many hours in the car w my brothers' farts

LINA:

lol yes obviously

sam do u want to ride with us too?

SAMIRA:

i'm actually not going

mama is letting me stay so i don't miss any more workshop

she even coordinated rides and stuff for me with farah

can u imagine lol

it's like i got a whole new mom

gabrielthepoet:

bookshelf & mocha this wknd?

we could even stay for the open mic if it's cool w ur mom

xo_samira_07:

omg yes

speaking of my mom

turns out she's so cool

i was just going about it all wrong

i'm learning all this stuff abt my grandpa also

will tell u in person

but yes yes yes

HORUS

eyeamhorus:

hey beautiful girl

i miss you

when can i see you again?

arimasamira:

hiiii

where are you these days

eyeamhorus:

i could be in dc, if you want

arimasamira:

idk

i mean of course i want to see you

but me and my mom just got back on good terms

and idk it would feel bad to do something behind her back

especially bc she's out of town

and is like trusting me enough to stay home alone

eyeamhorus:

who said anything about going behind your mom's back

you're the one that's keeping me a secret

i don't think we have anything to hide

are you ashamed of being with me?

arimasamira:

omg of course i'm not ashamed

it's not that at all

i just come from a really strict culture

and i'm not supposed to have a boyfriend or anything like that

so it isn't about you specifically at all

it's just about talking to any boy ever

eyeamhorus:

i would think i mean more to you than just "any boy ever"

i'm trying really hard to make this work samira

you ever notice that it's always me that has to come to you?

and now you won't even let me do that?

do you even want us to be together?

arimasamira:

wait what of course i do!!!

of course i do

i'm sorry

i really didn't mean to make it seem like this isn't important to me

and it means so much to me that you make the long trip to see me

ok let's try this again

yes i would love to see you

wanna go to the park again?

and then maybe we can get dinner after?

my mom is out of town so no curfew or anything

eyeamhorus:

i'd love to see where you live

arimasamira:

lol it's nothing special i promise

eyeamhorus:

still, i wanna see it

arimasamira:

if u insist lol

pick me up from here? i can give u a quick tour

then we'll go to the park

xo_samira_07:

ok i'm sooooo sorry but actually something came up

can't do bookshelf tomorrow

raincheck pls????

gabrielthepoet:

no worries at all

sending you my workshop poem now if u wanna send me urs

xo_samira_07:

yes 100%

kinda obsessed w pantoums these days

lmk if you have any favorites

i might try writing one for next workshop

gabrielthepoet:

check out this natalie diaz one

hold on let me get the link

Link: My Brother at 3 A.M. by Natalie Diaz

xo_samira_07:

yaaaay ur the best thank u

btw got my phone back

welcome me back to the world of the living!!!!!

THE COST

i've scrubbed the house until its every surface shines

& scented the air with incense.

i can't help but think mama would be proud

though, with a little ache, i realize she'd be the opposite of proud

that i am breaking her trust right after she finally gave it

that maybe i never deserved it at all

maybe i'm just as bad as they say

just as bad as she thought

or maybe even worse

but i have to put that thought away.

if this is the cost of an uninterrupted day with horus

to prove to him that i care

that he's not the only one trying to make this work

then i'll pay it

DOORWAY

the doorbell rings, & he is standing there, beautiful,
dropping his bags to the floor as his dark scent
of sandalwood surrounds me in his embrace
& his lips press firmly to mine

i can't believe i have him here, that i am kissing
him here, that i finally have him all to myself
no alibi, no ticking clock.
i take his hand & lead him inside

THE TOUR

he steps into the house
& inhales deeply.
it smells like you he murmurs
closes his eyes in sheer pleasure

i sweep my hand dramatically
around the room
well, this is it
i announce
kitchen, living room,
then the rooms are upstairs,
but this is basically it.
ready to go to the park?

but he is gazing at me
something flickering in his eyes.
trying to kick me out
so quickly, already?
he flashes me his half smile
& i relax once i realize
it's just a joke
& head toward the door.
actually, before we go,
could i get something to eat?
i'm pretty hungry
from the long bus ride

LEFTOVERS

i set the table & ladle out a bowl
of okra that mama left for me
glistening over its bed of rice

he groans with pleasure at the first bite.
samira, wow, just wow. you made this?
& i open my mouth to respond with the truth
but it doesn't feel right to invoke my mother
in this moment, doesn't feel right to remind
either of us that this is her house, that i am
her daughter, just a kid microwaving
her mother's cooking

so instead i nod, & he grins.
when are you going to move to new york already
so you can cook for me, & take care of me?

& i can picture it so clearly, our life
together, lived openly, when he will finally be
mine every day, beside me every day
no longer a secret, & maybe one day he'll even
come back here, to this house, when mama
isn't gone, maybe he'll sit with her
in the living room & drink tea & regale her
with stories of his travels, of his work
& she will warm at his brilliance, will tell him
about her father, about his library, & he will
tell her how much he loves me, everything
he sees in me, will say the word *forever,* & she
will give us her blessing

HORUS

when he's done eating he gets up from the table
leaving his empty bowl & crumpled napkin behind

i start to gather them & clear the table
when he calls to me from the couch

why don't you stop worrying about the dishes
& come over here?

& i put the bowl back down on the table
noticing, as if from very far away

the slight tremble in my hands

i take a breath & try to tamp down the nervousness
in my voice before i call back

yes, one second. hey, do you want to go to
a movie? what's your favorite?

probably something with subtitles,
am i right?

i chatter on frantically as i take my seat
beside him on the couch, & he calms me

by placing his hand on mine, his voice soft.
maybe later. will you look at me?

& i barely have time to turn my eyes to him
before his body presses over mine

HORUS

his kisses are usually soft, languid, luxurious
but now his every movement is urgent, frantic
his breathing ragged, his weight crushing the air
from my lungs, the taste of lamb & okra, usually
so familiar, all wrong on his breath

his hands travel first into my hair, grabbing
fistfuls that pull sharply at my scalp
& then his hands are everywhere

& i can't breathe, not with him pressed over me
like this, & without any air in my lungs
i can't make my voice come out at all

i feel dizzy, light-headed, & i claw at his chest
to ease him off of me, but he is stronger
& now i really can't breathe, & the panic
begins to take hold, the blood rushing away
from my limbs & leaving a sensation
like static, & i push harder at his chest

& the tears are here, hot & sliding down
the sides of my face, & still he won't get off
& i think i might be screaming now, but still
there is no air to give it sound, & my hands
reach up & find his face, & my fingernails
scrape hard, & i think i've broken skin

because he jolts away from me in a hiss
of pain & sits up, panting, & i scramble out
from underneath him, heaving loudly
for air, & he is grimacing & touching
his cheek, & when his hand pulls away
i see the small dots of blood

& this is all going so wrong, i don't
understand how it went wrong so quickly
& before i can say anything, before
i can apologize, he is hurrying off the couch
striding toward his bags & sliding them
over his shoulder, & when i finally find
my voice & call out to his retreating back

he turns around, briefly, something like disgust
etched all over his face, the small wound marring
his otherwise-smooth skin, & he shakes
his head, & his voice is quiet, so quiet

as he mutters *you really are just a kid*
& then the snap of the door shutting behind him
& then i am left alone, fully & truly alone

HORUS

i don't know how much time has passed
since he left, but i've only just caught
my breath, only just felt the blood
returning to my shaking limbs

i rise unsteadily from the couch
& go to clear the table, to wash
& stack the dishes, to drink a big glass
of water, then another, & another
followed by a long & scalding shower
& only then do i feel returned to myself

i reach for my phone, abandoned
for hours now, & see messages
from tam & lina (*WE MISS YOU!!!*)
from my mother (*hi habiba, checking in,*
there's okra for you in the fridge)
from farah (*hi samira, just confirming*
we're on for carpool on monday)
& absolutely nothing, anywhere
from horus

HORUS

his words follow me for days
they haunt me
& take on new & terrifying shapes

you really are just a kid

& i'm not, i want to let him know
that i'm not, i want to believe
that i am not, but his silence
makes the words echo even louder.
his silence drains the color from my days
drains them of all sense

mama & aunt aida return, cheerful
& their chatter washes over me
as a series of unrecognizable sounds

my texts from lina & tamadur accumulate
into the double digits, & i make myself
respond just enough to keep them
from asking questions

i go through the motions of my days
as if possessed, working my face into
something like a smile when mama
addresses me, replying to her questions
with words that feel impossibly far away

i just want to hear his voice
to speak to him & fill my brain
with new words to replace the awful
incantation he left behind

i cannot have those be the last words
he speaks to me

i cannot have those words be true

SAMIRA:

hey, i'm really sorry about what happened

any chance ur still in town?

this is samira btw

i got my cell phone back

in case u didn't guess from the 202 number :)

arimasamira:

i really am so sorry

could we just talk about it?

could u call me back?

xo_samira_07:

hi it's me

it's samira

why won't you answer the phone?

i just need to talk to you

please

- -

From: Samira Abdullahi <samira.abdul@whs.edu>
To: Horus EyeAm <eye.am.horus@email.com>
Subject: (no subject)

please can we talk

THE PLAN

despite everything that's happened
horus never actually took back his invitation
to open for him at the show next weekend
& i have to believe that's a kind of sign

& since i can't reach him any other way
maybe if i show up, maybe if i wear
the perfume oil he loves, the earrings
he got me, maybe we can talk about
what happened, & start to make it
make sense

maybe if i get onstage
& read the poem i wrote for him
maybe i can get him to give me
a few moments of his time
an explanation, a way to understand
how this was all a misunderstanding,
a miscommunication, & his words
will soothe my aching, twisting brain
now that some time has passed, maybe
i can reorient how i remember it. maybe
i was just nervous at the newness
of his touch, its urgency & heft, & i reacted
without thinking. & i must have hurt his feelings.
confused him. made him feel so rejected. hurt
him, dragged my fingernails along his cheekbone
& drew blood. maybe i should apologize

my poems are what brought him to me
in the first place, so i am going to show up
& i am going to read them perfectly, powerfully

i am going to show him i'm a serious artist
just like him, that i'm grown, just like him
not a kid, but a poet, a woman. maybe then
we can work this out

FREEWRITE

persephone to her lover

maybe you hate me
maybe i'm sorry
maybe i wasn't even there
maybe i fell out of my own body
and watched you grab at my shell
maybe you didn't see my eyes,
maybe i should pay attention,
to tell myself about this later

Samira,

On a craft level, I think this is maybe a fragment of something larger—it seems, at the moment, a little unfinished. Or, more specifically, it feels like the later part of a poem, and the earlier part is missing. Does that make sense?

    On a personal level, I know we don't usually discuss the content of the poems in here, and I want to respect that boundary. But I also want you to know that you can talk to me about anything, okay?

—Free

WORKSHOP

i sit, squirming in my chair
as farah's voice, which seems

so far away, rises & falls
as she talks excitedly about

something, maybe prose poems
i'm not actually sure, i'm barely

concentrating, shivering instead
in the air-conditioning, the touch

of cold air to my raw skin like
fingernails along an exposed nerve

you good?   gabriel whispers
beside me, placing his hand

on my forearm, & i snatch it
away, as if burned, tears announcing

themselves in my eyes   *fine*   i hiss
turning back to face farah   trying

my best to arrange my face
to seem attentive

HORUS:

all good

see you around

HORUS

at the sight of his name

on my phone, something drops

low in my stomach, clenches

in my chest, sends static down

my arms & legs, loosens my shoulders

with relief

his answer is vague

& unsatisfying

but i read & reread it dozens

of times, parsing it for meaning

scanning it like a poem, trying

to understand its music, its choices

"all good" could be a dismissal

or it could be forgiveness

acknowledgment of the misunderstanding

between us

"see you around" could be a dismissal

or it could be an invitation

a door cracked open

to let me know he's still on the other side

a dismissal & another dismissal

or forgiveness & an invitation

i comfort myself with the fact

that he hasn't disinvited me

from the show, the opening slot

so i choose to follow my own read

of this poem, to follow him

through the door

THE LIE

mama sits on the couch
one hand clicking through
channels for a movie to watch
the other patting the seat beside her
for me to join

i make my way toward the couch
but the sight of it, the feel of it
makes me feel like i'm going
to be sick, so i reroute & start
to lower myself into a chair

why so far? mama asks
you don't like the way i smell
or something? a smile creasing her eyes.
anyway, you can't really see the tv from there,
& i was thinking we could watch
one of the old halim movies

shoving away the memory, the sensation
i make my way onto the couch
mama reaching for my feet & gathering them
into her lap, a tenderness that would
usually cause an ache in the part of me hungry
to be mothered, muffled tonight by the clamor
in my head, the ringing in my ears

& i already hate myself for the lie i have
to tell her, but i'm running out of time
tomorrow looming with the last remaining hours
until the show. i promise myself this is
the last time, the absolute last time, before
i apply myself fully to the work
of deserving her, of being her girl

mama, can i still go to tam's thing tomorrow?
her cultural showcase? & with a loving squeeze
of her hand she says *of course* & i think she was right
before, that i've become someone she doesn't recognize
because i don't know that i even recognize myself

the light from the television glows blue against
our faces. i pull my feet from her lap, pretending
to stretch, & remain sitting upright instead. a different
kind of lie, i try to tell myself, to protect this new
& brittle return to each other. they almost bridge
the distance between us, the lies i tell myself
as i add my own name to the list
of people i am lying to

GABRIEL

GABRIEL:

are you ok?

you like stopped talking in workshop

and then you just run out right after

did i do something to upset you?

is something going on?

SAMIRA:

no no no of course you didn't do anything

just a lot on my mind

so so sorry

btw

i'm doing my first ever set

at bookshelf & mocha tomorrow

horus asked me to open for him

what poems do u think i should do

GABRIEL:

all your poems are great

but i think you should for sure do the persona poem

and the two list poems

THE PLAN

tam's show starts at 7, ends at 9
horus's show starts at 7, doors at 6:30

gabriel says to aim for 6
in case there's sound check

i tell tamadur i have a reading
with my workshop group

that i'll go first so i can be done early
so she gives me the closing slot

for her show, where i'll go on at 8:30
which gives me plenty of time

to finish one set before heading to the other

MIRROR

i look good, dressed all in black
with the earrings horus got me
hanging heavy as ripe fruit
from my ears

my eyeliner is dark, extended
in a cat-eye, kohl along my waterline
mascara thickening my curled lashes

i release my hair into its full power
perfumed & fluffed with a pick
hairline smoothed in cursive swoops
with gel & a toothbrush

mama only knows about tamadur's event
& has given me her permission, but i know
better than to push my luck, & instead
of applying my bright red lip
in front of the mirror & marveling in
the completed look, i stow it in my bag
for right before i take the stage

THE SHOW

though gabriel suggested arriving at 6
it took me three tries to get my cat-eye

exactly symmetrical, & the time has gotten
away from me, & by the time i walk in

the clock reads 6:45

inside the dimly lit room i wait for my eyes
to adjust & focus the silhouettes into faces

gabriel's familiar outline approaches,
teeth shining in a smile, & before i can greet him
i recognize the other figures behind him

all other poets from the workshop
farah stepping out from the back of the cluster
of bodies, also smiling, but with something
i can't read behind its surface

though when she speaks her voice is cheerful.
gabriel thought it would be great for us
to come out & support one of our own tonight

& his smile stretches even wider behind her
proud of his idea as he chimes in *yeah, i might even*
tell the host to just give you the headline slot

since we know who the best poet in tonight's lineup is
& i roll my eyes at him but can't tamp down my own
growing smile

after a quick round of hugs i break from the group
to look for horus, to apologize for being late

to apologize again for the other thing

& maybe find some time to be alone with him
before the show begins

6:50 PM

on tiptoes i scan the room for the familiar shape
of his hair, & when i can't find him i add another
text to the growing list of unanswered messages

hi! i'm here! looking for u
Delivered

through the milling crowd i notice a few silhouettes
exiting through a set of curtains to the left of the stage
& figure my best bet is to ask someone if he's
back there, explain that i'm the opener & if
he's backstage, could i maybe be let in as well?

i weave through the crowd where, as always,
everyone is taller than me, & finally, ducking
between two people, i emerge near the front
of the room to find him there, horus, whose own
stature has kept him hidden by the other bodies.
he is leaned up against the wall, his hand twisting playfully
in the long, curly mane of a girl whose back
is to me, whose back view makes me stare
for a long, confused moment

because from this angle, in this light, for that moment
before i can make any sense of what is happening,
the girl could be me. i move closer, stepping over
to see her face. & when i see it i take in the softness
of her jawline, the rounded shape of her adoring eyes
& i begin to understand

his lips are quirked upward in that half smile
i love, that i've come to think of as only mine
& the sick feeling moves from my stomach
to the dangerous base of my throat. because
not only is he not only mine—

because i know the gap between our ages
is forbidden, taboo. because he made me feel
like i was worth the risk, so special he had to break
every rule to call me his. but in this girl, smiling shyly
back up at him, in her face i see everything. the truth.
the faces of my classmates, of the others in the workshop
of a teenager. what he called *just a kid.* another girl my age

6:55 PM

i turn away from them, trying to swat
the image out of my head, to swallow the feeling
down into that hidden place where i keep all
my other questions about him, all
my other doubts. tonight, i am a professional.
a real poet. & i can't let this, or anything,
rob me of that chance

by the stage i see the host, hair locked in a long mane
down his back, clipboard in his hand. i approach
shyly at first, & when my meek *excuse me* is swallowed
by the chatter of the milling crowd, i clear my throat
& straighten my back, stepping closer & speaking clearly

excuse me, hi, i'm samira, i'm opening for horus
tonight & just wanted to let you know that i'm here
& apologize for being late & missing sound check
& everything, but i think whatever mic setup horus
is using should work fine for both of us, i don't know,
what do you think? i look up, losing my nerve in his
silence, waiting for recognition to smooth
his furrowed brow, but instead he shakes his head

leans over so i can just make out his voice through
the noise of the room around us, the roar of blood
in my ears, as he says *i'm really sorry, little sis, but we don't*
really do opening acts for our open mic features, unfortunately,
& horus never said anything about bringing another guest,
but i can offer you a spot on the open mic, if you'd like?

that way you can still get to share. & i think about saying no but in the crowd i see the shining faces of my workshop group of farah, gabriel, all assembled tonight for me, not horus only me, & i want to do it for them. i take the offered pen, steady it in my shaking hand. i print my name neatly at the top of the list

7:00 PM

farah, gabriel, & the others are crowded around two tables
in the front of the room, laughing & joking & glancing up
toward the stage in anticipation

i hang back, alone, in a corner, scanning every table
for horus, for that girl, & do not see them anywhere

he must have taken her with him backstage

i want so badly to talk to him, to let him soothe me
with his voice, his reasoning, the explanation he always
manages to pull smoothly from thin air

but it is as if i am at the edge of a dream, moments
from waking, the shapes dissolving & beginning
to reveal the red of the sun shining behind my closed eyelids

7:10 PM

the open mic begins, & still he has not emerged
to join the audience, still is not even standing
in the wings.

when my name is called i rise & float to the stage
barely feeling my own legs carrying me there
or my arms swinging heavily at my sides

& when i reach the stage the microphone is too high.
i fumble with it for a moment, & just when i think
it might be stuck, i remember farah mouthing to me

on that first night, *lefty loosey*. & with a twist the mic
slides down toward me, & with another i lock it into place.
i take a breath. & i know i can call him back to me

i settle again into that eerie calm, that perfect internal quiet.
i take another breath & begin:

i think i met all the wrong ones before you & i think
they ruined me but i think you're really handsome
the way a map is handsome—

& when i'm done i feel triumphant, breaking my head through
the surface of the poem, returning to myself. i take a large gulp
of air & look out into the room, but something is different.
something is not right.

there is a smattering of applause, mostly from
my workshop group, their hoots & cheers stark
against the quiet of the room. then the room falls silent
for a moment before erupting into the familiar hiss of whispers
soaking me in that familiar shame of knowing
i am being talked about. at first i don't know what it is
they think i've done wrong. then i hear words emerging
from the hiss, beginning to take shape
horus's poem   did she think we wouldn't
recognize it?   not sure who she thinks she is
just a kid   probably just a fan
& the truth snaps into place, too loud, too bright:
everyone thinks my poem is his.
all this time he's been passing it off
as his own, to an audience that adores him,
that believes him, that doesn't know me.
all this time he's been stealing from me
& i know it now, too late,
sweating under the bright lights of the stage
in front of a room full of people who think
i'm the thief

7:15 PM

i return to my corner in the back of the room
avoiding the table where i pretend
i can't see farah's attempts to catch my eye

i find a lone chair as the open mic continues in a blur
the words crossing such great distance to reach me
that by the time they've arrived
they are only sounds i can no longer decipher

but when the host returns to the stage
& begins to introduce horus
i feel my focus return
sharpening the room into unbearable colors
the hum of anticipation thickening in the air

horus is an internationally acclaimed poet
& performer whose accolades include . . .
i see his familiar silhouette in the wings
trying & failing to embrace the flurry
of motion that is the new girl's angry form.
i see her cross her arms & turn away from him
i see him lean in to murmur something into her ear
that i recognize even from his posture as an excuse.
she is still shaking her head & refusing him when the host
finishes his introduction & calls horus up to the stage
& now, all the way from brooklyn, new york city
the man you all came here to see, my good brother
the legend, horus
as he presses a quick kiss onto her forehead

8:00 PM

he waits until the room falls silent
then horus strides onto the stage in a pool of light.
he brushes his mouth close to the microphone
& i know it, that kiss, its memory twisting in my stomach.

horus stands astride the stage in a pool of light
& i know before i know that this is where it all goes wrong.
i still see it, that kiss, that other girl, & my stomach twists.
he opens his mouth & takes all the air from my lungs

i know before i know that this is where it all goes wrong.
horus squints into the crowd, his eyes alighting on my face.
he opens his mouth & takes all the air from my lungs:
my mentee, samira, is here tonight, she shared her remix of my poem

his smile gleams into the crowd, its light scorching my face.
let's give her another round of applause & claps his hands
to my mentee, samira, & to the next generation of poets.
my legs move as if disconnected from my brain, & i rise to my feet

another wave of applause as he clasps his hands together
& brushes his mouth close to the microphone.
my legs disconnect from my brain, blood pooling in my feet
i stand there until the room falls silent

8:10 PM

he launches into the poem, my poem, now known
to the whole world as his, & only his

i think i met all the wrong ones before you & i think
they ruined me but i think you're really beautiful

the way a map is beautiful—
& i can barely feel the silent pour of tears down my face

he finishes the poem & begins another.
i remember that i am standing because i need to leave

but the room is packed with bodies
crowded around booths, sitting on the steps to the stage

standing against the wall, blocking every doorway
every exit

& while at first they are rapt, held close
by the velvet of his voice, by the third poem

those sitting closest to me have begun to turn
their heads & stare, instead, at me

my wet face catching in the light

8:15 PM

just as the first sob rips from my throat
i feel a firm hand on my shoulder

i recognize farah by her bright scent of orange
blossoms, dark note of cigarettes underneath

she steers me outside, winding our way
through the parting crowd

& the air outside is humid & thick
heavy with the promise of rain

i do not recognize the sounds i am making
ugly, animal sounds, hoarse & jagged wails

farah has not spoken & continues, with a hand
on each of my shoulders, to steer

at the corner of 15th street
she nudges me to the right

until we reach the park
emptying in the quiet dusk

8:30 PM

she produces from her worn leather book bag
a stack of brown paper napkins
& when i've finished wiping my face they make
a darkened, crumpled pile on the bench between us

in a low voice, she begins
what do you need, samira? do you want to talk?
do you want me to talk? do you want a ride home?
i shake my head, & we sit awhile in silence
the city humming with its usual noises
just outside the park

for a long time we sit without speaking
the sounds of traffic settling into a sort of rhythm
that is almost soothing
buses sighing to a halt at the stops nearby
until i am finally ready to tell her everything

farah, i'm so embarrassed. i'm so ashamed.
& for a few moments this feels like all i can say
until i see her shaking her head.
samira, everyone in that room could see
that things were not as they seem
were not as he was telling them.
i know that poem was yours—

& i know she means to be reassuring
but i interrupt
it's not even about the poem, really, it's all of it.

my reputation is ruined, everywhere.
even in this new world i chose for myself.
i'm never going to be taken seriously as a writer,
as a poet. i've lost my name. i've lost my boyfriend.
i thought we were in love. he tricked me,
& he didn't even do it very well, but i still fell
for his whole thing. he would just lie, & i would
believe him even when i didn't believe him,

does that make sense? i kept trying to make him
into something that he was showing me he really
was not, but i'd already made my mind up
that he was the one for me, that i'd chosen him
& could not unchoose him, because everyone already
thinks such horrible things about me that i felt like

i just had to make it work, like making it work
with him would prove that i was a real poet or a serious
artist, & maybe later we could have even gotten
married or something, & then everyone would stop
talking about me.
& i just feel so unbelievably stupid

& now i feel the panic rising in my chest, settling
onto my lungs, until i am panting to catch my breath.
samira, breathe.
farah's voice is still low, more urgent now.
put your head between your knees & try to breathe.
& i feel almost outside my body
except for the tingling in my limbs
the blood coursing like static into my fingers, my feet

& as if from very far away i register the insistent vibration
of the phone in my pocket
but before i can think to reach for it
farah begins again to speak.
samira, i can tell people, i can put him on blast,
if you wanted that, i would do it.
i shake my head.
i just want my heart to not be broken

she nods, though through her quiet hum of sympathy
there is something else in her face
& slowly my breath returns to me, slowly the panic
drains from my body & leaves me wrung out & exhausted
& when farah again offers a ride home, i gratefully accept

MISSED

in the car i reach absently for my phone

i see, first, that the time is 9:45 pm

i see, second, calls & texts from gabriel
from everyone else in the workshop group

i see, third, eight missed calls from lina & messages
from her & our group chat in the double digits

fourth & last i see the twenty-five missed calls
from tamadur. i see her messages

& the panic finds its way down to my stomach

TAMADUR

farah's car approaches the community center
where every window is dark except for one
whose dim light shows the silhouette
of a lone figure inside stacking chairs

i thank farah for the ride & hurry in
to find tamadur dragging a tower of chairs
toward the edge of the room
everything silent except for the groan of metal
chair legs scraping against the linoleum floor

i rush to her, words & excuses
already pouring from my mouth.
tam, i'm so sorry, i'm so so so sorry.
i know you must really hate me right now,
but i swear i can explain everything.
i've had the most intense night,
you would not believe, i'll tell you
everything, just please give me
a chance to explain

& she will not look at me, will not speak.
she settles the stack of chairs against the wall
wipes the sweat from her brow
& begins dragging another.
the wail of metal against flooring
fills the air between us

LINA

tamadur still has not spoken
when another voice
rings out from the doorway.
samira, what is your problem?

i turn to see lina's round face
hardened by anger.
we know you've been avoiding us
all summer, we don't hear anything
from you unless we make the effort
to come out to see you, & then
you know this night was huge for tam,
& you know she's been talking
about it all summer, & then
you just flake on her

because you decide you have
something more important to do
with your weird old boyfriend
or your new poetry friends?
we're not your backup friends,
samira, you can't just dip in
& out of this when it's convenient
for you

here the firm set of her voice
breaks a little.

you're just so selfish,
so selfish,
& i'm done.
i've had more than enough

TAMADUR & LINA

lina.
tam.
my voice is hoarse
cracking along each
of their vowels

i know that's what it looks like.
i know i've been a terrible friend.
but please, just let me tell you everything

the whole truth this time

& then if you don't want to talk to me anymore
after this, i understand, but please
just let me tell you what's been going on

lina's fists are clenched at her sides
her stance refusing to soften
so i expect it to come from her
but it's tamadur who says, softly
sam, i need you to leave

RE:

From: Samira Abdullahi <samira.abdul@whs.edu>
To: Horus EyeAm <eye.am.horus@email.com>
Subject: please

you stole my poem i have screenshots of our messages i can prove that it's mine

i don't understand why you're doing this

please just tell everyone it's my poem horus please

From: Horus EyeAm <eye.am.horus@email.com>
To: Samira Abdullahi <samira.abdul@whs.edu>
Subject: Re: please

samira, i'm not sure what poem you're referring to. does your mother know i've been to her house?

THE COST

i understand it now

the shape, the nature of the cage

i've built for myself

with my secrets

with my lies

if i tell the world about horus

he'll tell my mother about me

about us

he'll prove to her that she was right

not to trust me

that she was wrong to give me a chance

this is the cost of my secrets

of my lies

the price i am being asked to pay

to keep them

is my silence

the price is to sign my words over

to him

MAMA

i feel like i've lost everything

my best friends, my boyfriend, my poem

my reputation, the real one:

my name as a writer, as an artist

the one i actually care about

& losing it hurts a thousand times more

than every time i've ever been called a bad girl

& i don't know what to do.

i've made every wrong choice

eaten every forbidden seed of pomegranate

trapped myself beneath the world of the living

& i've never felt more alone.

it's all my fault   i did it to myself

but i wish someone would help me

i am staring at mama's back

trying to communicate with her telepathically

while she stirs something on the stove

help me   help me   please   i need your help

& she does not turn around

& i can't really ask her, can't really tell her

without losing her as well

i entered into a contract without first

understanding the rules, without knowing

that eating from the fruit would bind me

to the underworld, to a darkness, a cage

& now i can't leave

i can't ever return

to the warmth & light of my former life

its beautiful simplicity

i give up & flop, exhausted, onto the couch

reaching for my book, tented open on the table to save the page

when i hear her voice float over from the kitchen

where are tamadur & lina these days?

why don't you ask them over to dinner?

& i'm halfway up the stairs before the sob

wrenches from my throat

SAMIRA:

i know you're still mad at me and i get it

i know i messed up

and i know i don't deserve to be your friend

but i miss you both so much

and i'm so sorry

i'm really so sorry

i don't know who i am without you

like

being your friend is part of my identity

and now i feel like i'm just floating in space

like i'm not anybody anymore

5

In tears, [Persephone] called her mother, called
Her comrades too, but oftenest her mother.

—OVID, *METAMORPHOSES*

FREEWRITE

what i've learned

my body is a pill
small
& love is the wrong man's tongue
to tell me so

my body dissolves
my body finds a man who is water
& calls him home

my body is everything
that happened to me
love is what my body borrows
to forget
love is a pill
my body is water

my body is a tongue
& love dissolves
love calls the wrong man home
love makes my body a stain
& goes looking for water
on the wrong man's tongue

love is a house
my body is a bath drawn in floodwater
my body trickles in through the floorboards
love is the carpet that i ruin

love is decoration
is an alternative to water
is just something to do until the wars start

my body is a border
drawn up by some man long ago
love is everything
that happened in between
love is the floorboards

my body is decoration
love ruined all the carpets
my body is the carpet
my body is the stain
love makes it all dissolve
love is an alternative to home
love is floodwater

my body burned to the ground
my body called the wrong man home
love started the fire
my body is everything
that happened after

the wrong man is an alternative to love
the wrong man is a map
home is where he puts the lines
my body is a border drawn by accident
by the wrong man's tongue
love makes scars on my body
& calls them borders

the wrong man mistakes my body
for a body of water
love let the wrong man decide
what my body mistakes for home
love started the fire

my body is a house on fire
my body drew a bath in floodwater
the wrong man is floodwater
love & the wrong man
are an alternative to hating my body
my body is a body of water
poured over everything that happened to me
my body makes every scar an island
the wrong man makes my body small
a pill
love makes the water
& my body dissolves

RE:

From: Gabriel Diop <gdiop@cdhs.edu>
To: Samira Abdullahi <samira.abdul@whs.edu>
Subject: Re: "what i've learned" (poem)

sam this is really beautiful, and the form is really wild—is it
invented? it has big sestina vibes but i can't quite place the
pattern.

also, i know we're not really supposed to ask about the content of
the poems but is this about that dude? i know you must be going
through so much and i don't want to ask you about anything you
don't want to talk about, but if you ever do want to talk about it, i
want you to know that i'm here, and that i got you.

also, everyone from workshop knows that poem was yours. we
know your work. i know your work. he's not gonna get away with
this. if you want to fight, we can fight this. you have people, samira.

g

THE FORUM

i'm trying to find an old draft of a poem
to show to gabriel, who might be my only friend

these days, though all i can stand to talk about
with him is poetry, & he's careful not to ask

about anything else. but i can't find the poem
anywhere, not in my notebook, or in my phone

or anywhere on the computer
& just as i am about to text him

& admit defeat, the memory stirs, & i see myself
ages ago, typing it directly into the text field

on the poetry forum, where i haven't been
in months. i type in my password

& the familiar blue page loads before me
the endless scroll of white text boxes full of poems

& it pulls me immediately back in
though i've barely clicked through two poems

when a large block of writing appears next
no line breaks or stanzas or paragraph breaks

just a breathless tumble of text
& that's when i see his name

THE POST

____itstiaaaa:

i know ive probably been quiet about this for too long but its
time we all talked about HORUS and his slimy ways because
first of all not only is he just ALWAYS dating some teenage
girl (????) (me included unfortunately) he has also been
PLAGIARIZING WORK i was at this poetry event over the
summer in dc with him and this thing happened where a girl
read a poem on the open mic that was basically that poem of his
called love poem (which he told me he wrote for me but even i
am not that stupid lol) and everyone thought she stole it from
him but then he got onstage and called her his mentee and said
she had remixed his poem and then he read his version of the
poem but idk something immediately felt OFF but anyway that's
not even strike one, strike one is that this man is in his ENTIRE
twenties and i was fifteen when we first met and he did this thing
where he made me feel like i was so special that he had to risk
it all for me but then that other girl got up and started crying
during his set literally just stood there crying until everyone in
the room started looking at her instead of him until another girl
dragged her outside and you know how sometimes your gut just
TELLS you? i know they had something going on and this girl
was definitely my age or somewhere around it so why is it that we
have this grown man and so far the count is TWO teenage girls?
what he did to her was wrong and what he did to me was wrong
and idk i mostly just want to hear someone else say it back bc its
not right none of it is right and i am tired of keeping quiet about
this so i wanna know what are we gonna do about it

THE CHOICE

before i can change my mind
before i can use the implications
to talk myself back into the silence

before remembering horus's threat
& weighing again the cost of revealing
what was done to me

before believing once again that this
will lose me everything
except my voice, my words

before i can fall back into thinking
that i am willing to pay in silence to be loved
that i am willing to keep myself small

& unremarkable, commit myself to a lifetime
of wrenching myself into the shapes
of a more respectable daughter

i make my decision. i take a breath.
i release it. i take another. & before
i can change my mind again, i post

the screenshots. i choose, for the first time,
myself

arimasamira:

you hear this probably every day lol but i still have to tell u

i love your poems so much

would u ever be down to show me some of your writing?

something the rest of the world hasn't seen yet :)

eyeamhorus:

why don't you show me some more of yours?

or, even better, why don't you write me something?

arimasamira:

horus

i think i met all the
wrong ones before
you and i think they
ruined me but i
think you're really
handsome the way
a map is handsome,
with skin wide open
soaked in the whole
world's ink. i
think i'm done pulling
paint off the walls i

think i want to read
you the names of
every city that ever
burned down, i think
we'd like it there

it's ok if u don't like it i just kind of pulled it

out of nowhere lol don't read too much into it

u still there?

eyeamhorus:

beautiful

wow

samira

i don't even know what to say

this is the most beautiful thing i've ever read

no one's ever made me feel this way

arimasamira:

wow i'm so glad

you took long enough

i was convinced you hated it

eyeamhorus:

we should meet

arimasamira:

Link: Horus - LOVE POEM (new)

did you think i wouldn't find out?

eyeamhorus:

are you there?

i didn't want to have to call your house

but i have to talk to you

hello?

arimasamira:

please stop

i'm here but please stop calling

i'm going to get in so much trouble

we can talk here

eyeamhorus:

samira, i swear i gave you credit

i said

"this is a remix of a poem by a brilliant poet, who is also my girlfriend"

i said

"it's a poem she wrote for me"

"& it meant so much to me that i had to share it with you all"

you're my muse

i thought you knew that

arimasamira:

but it doesn't say that anywhere in the video

the video is just you reading my exact poem

with like two words changed

eyeamhorus:

whoever took that video didn't start recording until after i said that

i had no control over that

i would never steal from you

i actually can't believe you thought that i would steal from you

your "exact poem with like two words changed"

is that really what you think of me?

FREE

i spend what feels like hours
reading every single reply
to the first girl's post
& at the very bottom of the page
i see another block of text
& i recognize the name

freepoetry:

when i first left home i went to new york, and i met him there
through the local poetry community. and at all the events he
always had a much younger girl with him but no one ever said
anything about it. the one time i asked, someone literally referred
to it as *family business.*
i was working as a teaching artist and as a gift to my first-ever
poetry class, i got them all tickets to go to the local friday night
open mic and slam, and horus was the feature that night.
the host let each of my students read on the open mic. one of my
students, we'll call her X, who i secretly thought of as a rising star,
just super talented, she read a poem that the whole room loved,
standing ovation and everything, and afterward horus came up to
talk to all of us but spent an exceptionally long time talking to X.
the following week, X didn't show up to workshop, and i never
saw her again, she never responded to any of the maybe 25 emails
i must have sent her over the course of that year, but the next
time i caught one of horus's sets, a lot of his new poems sounded
like her work.

i tried to talk to the host of the venue, the local community of
poets, the program where i taught where he was an alum, but
no one seemed to want to believe me about him because he was
their golden boy, the most successful poet to come out of their
scene in recent history (acting roles in major films and tv shows,
commercials, commissions, etc.).
the community started to feel unwelcoming to me and closed
ranks around him, so i came back to dc to get away from him,
and over the years i've heard the same whispers but he keeps
getting away with it. i should have spoken up sooner. i should
have done more. and then he did it to another one of my
students, a different girl, a different city.
and i thought i was respecting her wishes by not calling him
out right there, not telling everyone. but i can't keep being a
bystander. something needs to be done.

FREEWRITE

i met him on the internet. he was a poet—is a poet. well-known. i was ashamed of being judged by my community, of being cast out, so i had no one to talk to about it. i had no one to tell me it was wrong . . .

THE BILLBOARD

mama, aunt aida, & i are walking
eight long blocks to the movie theater

it's been a day since i shared
my screenshots, vowing to myself
that i'd just post & walk away
without sticking around to see
the reactions, the comments,
that it was more important
to share my truth than spend
hours reading other people's
responses—
& still no call from horus.
no messages, no delivery
on his threat.
still mama doesn't know.

mama insisted on finding street parking
despite the heat, firm in her belief
that the prices for the garage are theft

she & aunt aida have the same exchange
every time, as if following a script

aunt aida says *this is ridiculous, in this heat?*
please, just let me pay for it.
& mama sets her jaw, shakes her head, says
it's the principle of the thing

& so we walk. the plan is to watch
something subtitled & slow that aunt aida
recommended we see together
despite the initial bickering
they seem closer than i've ever
seen them, chattering easily, each fixing
the other's hair & collar, naming possible
cuisines for lunch, comparing the snacks
they've smuggled in their purses,
sweating & cheerful in the sun

the walk is long & winding, a left turn here
a traffic circle, another turn. aunt aida mutters
to herself that we'll never remember where
we left the car, & mama pretends not to hear her

& when we finally reach the last corner to turn
the gasp catches in my throat

aunt aida & mama are debating whether
or not the nearby hot dog stand is really halal
& do not realize at first that i am frozen
in place, gaping

at a giant billboard, the familiar shape
of his hair, his body arched & triumphant
in a bright pair of sneakers, beneath the words
POETRY IN MOTION

they are watching me now, my mother
& my aunt, the question identical
on their faces

i take a breath. i take another. i turn to face them
the billboard at my back, & i begin
to undo my silence

TELLING

actually, can i read you something?
i ask, making myself look directly
into each of their faces, the only
resemblance between them the twinned
concern in each pair of eyes

& even through the sensation of my heart
knocking painfully in my chest, the air
going thick with tension in my lungs
i can understand how much they love me,
worry for me, have time for me, because
neither one brings up the fact that i am going
to make us late for the film

mama is the first to sit, perching herself
on the steps leading up to the theater
motioning to aunt aida to join her.

aunt aida, dressed in crisp white linen trousers
lowers herself beside mama
without hesitation

i pull the piece up on my phone
i take a breath in
i take another
& i begin

i met him on the internet. he was a poet—is a poet. well-known. i was ashamed of being judged by my community, of being cast out, so i had no one to talk to about it. i had no one to tell me it was wrong . . .

. . . i was not the whistleblower. i was just the girl who came before her, sistered to each other by this violation.

MAMA

for a long time they are silent
mama's downcast eyes intent
on her twisting hands, aunt aida
watching her, waiting for her
to speak first

samira
mama begins
her voice catching
her eyes rising to meet mine

she is not angry, is not
wailing & slapping her face
like she did in the past
when she learned
of my wrongdoing, alleged
& otherwise

her voice is very quiet
her eyes completely dry
& still i can see she is in pain
enormous pain, her voice
cracked & dry as ruined earth

samira, i'm so sorry i made you feel
like you couldn't come to me

i'm sorry i was so busy trying
to govern you, to protect you only
from the dangers i could imagine
for making you feel like you couldn't
come to me for help

i never meant to make you afraid of me.
i'm so sorry he used your fear of me
to trap you, to steal from you.
he is at fault here, but so am i

i want to make you a promise
need to make you a promise
that you can always come to me

i don't care what it is, i promise
any time you need me
you can come to me for anything
& that i am always on your side
whatever happens

the last thing i wanted was to be someone
you needed to hide from, someone
you no longer knew how to need

& i need you too, samira. we are in this
together. equal footing. no more secrets
born of fear. you will have me forever,
whatever you need. i will always come get you.
i will always choose you first

she & aunt aida rise from the stairs
in one fluid motion, like a single animal
& surround me with their embrace
& i am back inside my family, inside
their love, inside my enormous belonging

THE RETURN

& just like in the myth i feel the sun
return to touch my face, my eyes
adjusting to the yellow light

everything that lay dormant
in my grief finally emerging
from that long gray sleep
& putting out hopeful & tiny leaves

i will remember always this september
three months from seventeen
when my life's seasons were redone

winter replacing the three months others
knew as summer

spring arriving in my world just as
the world outside begins its work
of gold & orange

the bright blue of the sky marred only
by two clouds, two of my great loves
still missing, still yet to be restored

& so even in my season of light
my season of return
i grieve

SAMIRA:

i know it's too much to ask you to forgive me

after what i did

after how i've been acting

but i wrote something

and maybe you could read it

and maybe it'll help explain what's been going on all summer

SAMIRA:

ok here it is

you don't have to respond or anything

but i hope you'll still read it

i love you both so much

i'm so so so so sorry

i'm gonna spend the rest of my life trying to deserve u again

RE:

- -

From: Farah Abdelmounim <free.poetry@email.com>
To: Samira Abdullahi <samira.abdul@whs.edu>
Subject: Re:

Samira,

This is incredibly brave (and beautifully written). I'm so, so proud of you.

PS: Maybe this is too early, but this could be the bones of a really strong college admissions essay.

———

Farah "Free" Abdelmounim
Teaching Artist, Teen Poetry Workshop
Wednesday Open Mic Host, Bookshelf & Mocha
Poet & Performer

THE VISIT

i let myself into the house, calling out

to mama that i'm home, & as i fumble
with the laces on my shoes, she responds

from the living room *i'm going to some
ziyaras, but i invited some people over*

*who i think you might have been wanting
to see.* & the hope is too big for my body

& makes my knees shake as i pad into the room
my downcast eyes on my mismatched socks

the sight of them might be too much to bear
& it'll be unbearable if it isn't them

i gulp down a breath, then another, then
a third, before finally looking up

into tamadur's & lina's faces, so familiar
it makes my stomach ache, their sameness

their faces arranged politely in the presence
of my mother, but i know those faces better

than i know anything, & i see the wariness
behind their eyes, & it breaks my heart again

that i did this, that their hesitation where usually
there has only been ease between us

their carefulness, their formality, their politeness
all of it is my fault

mama drops a kiss on the top of my head
as she busies herself toward the front door

rummaging in her purse for her car keys
& calling out about leftovers in the fridge

when she shuts the door behind her she leaves
the three of us in a silence i know i have to be

the first to breach. we stand this way, across
the room from each other, as i begin to speak

AWAKE

even though i've sent them my piece
& think they must have read it, since they're here

i want to tell them everything, every detail
every sensation, everything i didn't quite

have words for, even as i was writing
i want to exorcize every secret, every silence.

aside from the gradual loosening of lina's
clenched fists, at first they do not move.

when i get to the part about horus & my poem
his excuse about a remix, lina's fists clamp shut again

tamadur sucks in a breath, but still they say nothing
they let me fill the silence with the story, the whole story

& as i tell it i begin to see its shape, begin to understand
the depth of the violation, of what was done to me

*& none of us have ever had a boyfriend, because it's not
allowed, so at first when things started to go bad*

*i didn't know if it was just regular relationship stuff,
& i think there was a part of me that thought*

*i was being punished for breaking the rules, that this
was what i deserved for being bad, for being shameful*

& now i am crying again, a fresh store of tears unlocked
as the story unfurls into the room around us

& he trapped me in my own secrets. he isolated me
from everyone. & i let him at first because i thought

we were in love, & then because i guess
i believed i deserved it

& i have no more words, & that ugly wail
is pouring out of me again

& tamadur & lina are around me in an instant
the warm crush of their embrace

my tears soaking into lina's t-shirt, which i faintly
register to be my t-shirt, tamadur stroking my hair

& wishing a stream of elaborate curses on horus
& i've finally woken up

from the end of my long winter
& i've finally come home

RE:

From: Farah Abdelmounim <free.poetry@email.com>
To: Samira Abdullahi <samira.abdul@whs.edu>
Subject: Re:

Hey Samira,

I have a few updates about the situation—the grapevine seems to be working, and there's a quiet network fighting to take him down. It might not look like much, but I do know there's an all-girls school that just canceled his annual workshop visit, and I have some friends at a few venues who have agreed not to book him. Let's think of it as a good start, but I know we're all hoping for more.

Let me know how you're doing?

Free

Farah "Free" Abdelmounim
Teaching Artist, Teen Poetry Workshop
Wednesday Open Mic Host, Bookshelf & Mocha
Poet & Performer

SUNDAY SCHOOL

after a soft knock on my since-reinstalled
bedroom door, mama asks if i want to join her
downstairs for some tea, for a movie

i click shut the computer, where i've finally
begun checking the notifications
on my screenshots post, which have accumulated
in the hundreds, other girls coming forward
with stories of their own, screenshots
of their own

in the kitchen mama is boiling the water
crushing fragrant pods of cardamom
with the flat end of a knife, arranging
ginger cookies onto a plate

i have some news she begins
an unfamiliar shyness in her voice
& i join her at the counter as she continues
placing sticks of cinnamon & little seeds
of clove into the painted teapot

i'm sure you've heard, but your friend mazin
& his family went back to sudan, leaving no one
to teach the sunday arabic classes, so some
of the parents have asked me to step in

not quite it, but something close to my original
dream of becoming a professor. she grins

trying to make it into a joke, but something soft
& hopeful is catching in her voice

& i know you've had a tough time there,
so i'm not saying you have to start going again,
but i wanted you to know that if you did want to go,
if you do, you will have me there with you,
& anyone who wants to say anything
will have to say it to my face

PERSEPHONE

in my rereading of the myth
the mother is imperfect in her grief

destructive, all-consuming
in her grief

but who wouldn't be if they found themselves
in her place?

& the man, we cannot know for sure
if he ever loved her, the girl

or if he only wanted something living
to rule over

& i've seen some try to shape romance
from that taking, to call it passion,

the girl so beautiful
he had to act at first sight

but why couldn't he
have just asked her?

have come to her in her field
of flowers & sat with her there

instead of the dark chariots
the underworld

the trick hidden in the fruit?

& the girl, throughout history
is still silent

a blank space for us all to color in
with whatever we already believe

RE:

From: Gabriel Diop <gdiop@cdhs.edu>
To: Samira Abdullahi <samira.abdul@whs.edu>
Subject: Re: "what i've learned" (poem)

samira,

not sure if i've told you about this already, but some friends and i have started an online literary journal, and i would really really love to publish your poem WHAT I'VE LEARNED in our first issue. i still can't stop thinking about the form. and if you want to send any other poems for consideration, you can just email them directly to me! (although yes we are fancy and official and have an actual Submittable page and everything)

also, i've been thinking, now that the workshop is over, maybe we can keep our own little workshop going with some of the other poets? we can also start sending work out to journals and magazines and stuff together. my dad always says that that's a good way to share your writing but keep it protected. the internet is kinda the wild wild west when it comes to posting your work. did i mention he's in town these days? we've been hanging out. i even showed him some poems! he said they "showed promise" lol but give me a couple more weeks and i swear i'll get a real compliment out of him.

anyway, let me know?

g

PS: the horus story is really making the rounds on the poetry internet. it was really brave, what you did.

MAMA

my mother is in the kitchen
misting water over the new
potted herbs, thriving
on the windowsill
singing quietly to herself

she is glowing, backlit
by the golden autumn sun
haloing itself around the lush darkness
of her hair

i stand awhile & watch her
a question on my lips
but i am reluctant to interrupt
the softness of the moment

she turns to me with a smile
you think you can sneak up on me?
i can smell that perfume oil on you
from a mile away

we share our laugh
then i take a breath
& begin to ask my question

mama?

yes, samira?

can i go to an open mic tomorrow?
it's at bookshelf & mocha
i'd be going with tam, lina
& my friend gabriel from workshop
only one boy—

she holds up a hand to stop me
& the rest of the words go quiet
in my throat

my pulse quickens with the memory
of every other time we've had this exchange
my old incantation starting up in my head

(please)   (please)   (please)   (please)

she shakes her head
& the motion strikes me in the part
of the memory that aches

but she's smiling

of course you can go
i'm glad to see you getting back out there
& no need for the head count
i trust you, remember?
let your aunt aida know if you'll need her
to drive you

i throw my arms around her
& plant a quick kiss

on the top of her head
thank you mama
you're the best

& as i free her from my arms
the idea strikes me
in a hot spark of inspiration

hey, would you want to come too?

Samira Abdullahi
Admissions Essay
University of New York

Everyone wants me to blame religion, my mother, the country in flames behind us, but I was not an unhappy child. We danced and colored and folded little paper boats to float in the bathtub. We tried our best and locked the doors and installed sensors in the windows. If I am to blame, it is only because I was forever curious, forever climbing onto the sill to peer out the locked window at the lives continuing outside. I was not unhappy, only restless. Only hungry to know what we were trying to keep out. It was I who opened the doors, the windows. It was I who let him into the house.

I met him on the internet. He was a poet—is a poet, a well-known one. I was ashamed of being judged by my community, of being cast out, so I had no one to talk to about it. I had no one to tell me it was wrong.

I was not the whistleblower. I was just the girl who came before her, sistered to each other by this violation. I was not the one who made it right, who said anything. But can it be enough that I'm saying it now?

OPEN MIC

my name is called & i make my way
to the stage, aware of the room full
of eyes on me, my arms swinging heavily
at my sides

& when i reach the stage the microphone is
as usual, too high, but with a twist to the left
it slides down toward me
& with a twist to the right i lock it into place

i close my eyes & take a breath
hands clutching my notebook
i open them to an array of beaming faces
crowded around a single table by the stage
shining, familiar faces

tamadur & lina
gabriel & farah
aunt aida & mama

& i settle into that perfect calm
that perfect internal quiet

i take another breath & begin

ACKNOWLEDGMENTS

To my poetry communities, who met me as a shy teenager and made me into a poet with their care and attention and camaraderie: thank you. For teaching me, for welcoming me, for giving me something to call myself.

To my many teachers and mentors, lateral and vertical, thank you for answering my questions, for your patience and rigor. Thank you for taking me seriously.

To every young poet: I hope you find your people, as I found mine. I hope you'll be better protected than I was, louder than I was, believed.

Thank you to Elizabeth Acevedo, Clint Smith, Eve Ewing, Fatimah Asghar, and Alison C. Rollins, who read years' worth of drafts of these poems. Thank you for the writing groups, the retreats, the accountability emails and check-ins and notes and encouragement.

To my poets. Thank you for finding me. Thank you for keeping me. Thank you, thank you.

MAKE ME A WORLD

A NOTE FROM CHRISTOPHER MYERS

Dear Reader,

On one hand, there are girls everywhere. Sleeping beauties and fire starters, police procedurals and teen comedies, plucky detectives and innocents lost. Solar systems' worth of stories revolve around images of girlhood.

On the other hand, girls are nowhere to be found. The sleeping beauty's job is to sleep and be beautiful. The fire starter is to be hunted by conflicted government agents. Police procedurals focus on the police; teen comedies focus on the romantic fumblings of teens. Plucky detectives function as devices to unearth other people's mysteries, and every innocent lost is a blank space upon which the desires and anxieties of storytellers are inscribed. The solar system spins around a blank space, a wishing well, a universe of stories made from the erasure of girls' voices.

Just as every story is a part of a longer conversation, an exchange of stories stretching back to the first moments when we asked ourselves who we are—the skeleton of this absence is very old.

What does it look like to throw off this centuries-old habit?

I think it might look something like *Bright Red Fruit*.

Samira carries the imaginations of so many people.

She sees herself through the eyes of her family, her community, her school, and the weight of all this vision is heavy. So when she sees herself through the eyes of Horus, for a moment it feels liberating. But as with so many visions, these eyes threaten to crowd out her own vision of self.

And this might be the challenge for every girl, for every young person, for every Jo and Dolores, Celie and Fa Mu Lan, to supplant all the imaginations pressing on their lives and find their way to seeing themselves.

The world's imagination is a heavy burden, and every young girl carries it. Here is a book to help in the carrying, a guide of sorts, one girl's journey, navigating the weight of the world's imagination on her endless shoulders.

Christopher Myers

ABOUT THE AUTHOR

Safia Elhillo is the author of the YA novel-in-verse *Home Is Not a Country,* which was longlisted for the National Book Award and received a Coretta Scott King Author Honor and an Arab American Book Award. She is also the author of the poetry collections *Girls That Never Die,* which was a national bestseller, and *The January Children,* which received the Sillerman First Book Prize for African Poets and an Arab American Book Award.

Sudanese by way of Washington, DC, Safia is a Pushcart Prize nominee, co-winner of the 2015 Brunel International African Poetry Prize, and listed in Forbes Africa's 2018 "30 Under 30." She lives in Los Angeles.

SAFIA-MAFIA.COM

DON'T MISS:

"NOTHING SHORT OF MAGIC."
—Elizabeth Acevedo, New York Times bestselling author of The Poet X

LONGLISTED FOR THE NATIONAL BOOK AWARD
WINNER OF THE ARAB AMERICAN BOOK AWARD FOR YOUNG ADULTS
A CORETTA SCOTT KING AWARD HONOR BOOK

"A love letter to anyone who has ever been
an outsider, or searched to understand their history,
no matter where they come from."
—NPR

3 STARRED REVIEWS!